THE BRIDES *of* BELLA ROSA

Romance, rivalry and a family reunited.

For years Lisa Firenze and Luca Casali's sibling rivalry has disturbed the quiet, sleepy Italian town of Monta Correnti, and their two feuding restaurants have divided the market square.

Now, as the keys to the restaurants are handed down to Lisa and Luca's children, will history repeat itself? Can the next generation undo their parents' mistakes, reunite their families and ultimately join the two restaurants?

Or are there more secrets to be revealed?

The doors to the restaurants are open, so take your seats and look out for secrets, scandals and surprises on the menu!

Turn to page 5 for **Diana Palmer's** secret recipe for the Bella Rosa sauce!

Thank you for your SUPPORT.

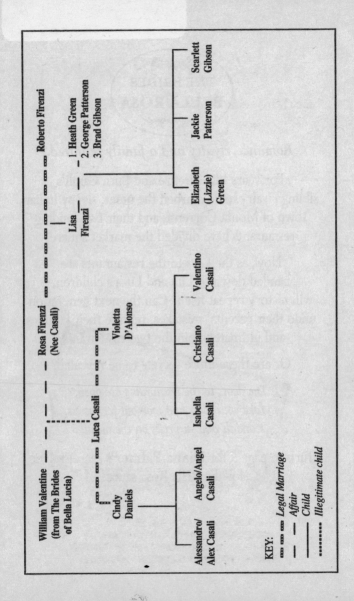

KEY: --- _Legal Marriage_   – – – _Affair_   —— _Child_   •••••• _Illegitimate child_

William Valentine (from The Brides of Bella Lucia) – – – Luca Casali

Rosa Firenzi (Nee Casali) – – – Roberto Firenzi

Lisa Firenzi

Violetta D'Alonso

Cindy Daniels

Alessandro/Alex Casali

Angelo/Angel Casali

Isabella Casali

Cristiano Casali

Valentino Casali

Elizabeth (Lizzie) Green

Jackie Patterson
1. Heath Green
2. George Patterson
3. Brad Gibson

Scarlett Gibson

RAYE MORGAN

Beauty and the Reclusive Prince

THE BRIDES
of
BELLA ROSA

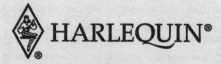

HARLEQUIN®

TORONTO • NEW YORK • LONDON
AMSTERDAM • PARIS • SYDNEY • HAMBURG
STOCKHOLM • ATHENS • TOKYO • MILAN • MADRID
PRAGUE • WARSAW • BUDAPEST • AUCKLAND

Recycling programs
for this product may
not exist in your area.

ISBN-13: 978-0-373-17650-2

BEAUTY AND THE RECLUSIVE PRINCE

First North American Publication 2010

Copyright © 2010 by Harlequin Books S.A.

Special thanks and acknowledgment are given to Raye Morgan
for her contribution to The Brides of Bella Rosa series.

Harlequin Romance reader favorite Diana Palmer would like to share her secret tomato sauce recipe with you. Diana grows her own herbs and tomatoes and she and her husband love to cook with them. Enjoy!

Tomato Sauce

Begin with a nice basket of organically grown plum tomatoes (about 2.6 lb) or equivalent cans of organic plum tomatoes, and a nice big bunch of fresh black basil. Wash tomatoes and cut into quarters.

Put 2-3 tablespoons of extra virgin olive oil into a pan; add 3-4 cloves chopped garlic. When garlic softens throw in the tomatoes. Simmer until tomatoes begin to soften, add a big handful (about 12 large leaves) of torn basil leaves. Add salt and pepper to taste.

Simmer sauce until tomatoes soften completely and slowly bring to the boil. Turn off heat and run sauce through a sieve or food mill for a smooth consistency. Or leave in the bits for a rough and ready pasta sauce.

When cool, add the Bella Rosa secret ingredient— 1 teaspoon of orange-infused olive oil and 1 teaspoon grated orange zest.

The sauce can be used alone, or as a base.

CHAPTER ONE

"ENOUGH!"

Isabella Casali's cry was snatched right out of her mouth by the gust of wind that tore at her thick dark hair and slapped it back against her face. What a night she'd picked to go sneaking onto royal property. The moon had been riding a crest of silky clouds when she'd started out from the village. Now the sky had turned black and the moon was playing hide and seek, taking away her light just when she'd stepped on forbidden territory. Where had this sudden storm come from, anyway?

"Bad luck," she whispered to herself, squinting against another gust of wind. "I've got reams of it."

She knew she ought to turn and head for home, but she couldn't go back without finding what she'd come for—not after all she'd done to work up the nerve to come in the first place.

The grounds of the local prince's palazzo were famously said to be the stomping grounds for all sorts of supernatural creatures. She'd discounted it before, thought it was nothing but old wives' tales. But now that she'd come here and seen for herself, she was beginning to get the shivers just like everyone else. Every gust of wind, every snapping twig, every moan from the trees made her jump and turn to see what was behind her.

"You'd better hope the prince doesn't catch you."

Those words had made her smile when Susa, her restaurant's vintage pastry chef, had uttered them like an aging Cassandra just before Isabella had left for this adventure. Susa often had wise advice, but this time Isabella was sure she was off the beam. What had Susa said again?

"They say he patrols the grounds himself, looking for young women who stray into his woods…"

"Oh, Susa, please," she'd scoffed. "They've said the same thing about every prince who's lived in that old moldy castle for the last hundred years. The royal Rossi family has never been a very friendly bunch, from what I've heard. When you don't get out and mix with the citizens, you're bound to get a bad reputation."

She'd chuckled at the time, completely unconcerned, even though the royal grounds were the last place she wanted to venture onto anyway. Given a choice, she would have stayed home with a good book.

"But it's mostly because they're such a mystery," she continued, thinking it over. "I'll bet they're very nice people once you get to know them."

Susa raised her eyebrows and looked superior. "We'll see how nice you think he is when he has you locked up in his dungeon."

"Susa!" Isabella was reluctant enough to go on this mission without the older woman raising more reasons why she should just stay home.

"Besides, Papa has been sneaking in there to collect the *Monta Rosa Basil* we need for years and, as far as I know, he's never seen a royal person there yet. I don't believe a word of it."

Her father, Luca Casali, had discovered the almost magical properties of this fine herb years before and it had transformed his cuisine from average Italian fare into something so special people came from miles around just to get a bowl of exquisitely cooked pasta topped with the steaming tomato-based sauce Luca had come up with.

The special recipe and the herb were a closely held family secret. Only a few knew that the delicious flavor came from a plant that could be found only on a hillside located on the estate of the royal Rossi family in Monta Correnti.

For years, her father had gone once a month to collect the herb. Now he was ill and could no longer make the trip. It was up to Isabella to take up the mantle as herb-gatherer, reluctant as she might be. She'd decided she might have less risk of being caught at it if she went at night. She was a little nervous, but fairly confident. After all, her father had never had a problem. She told herself calmly that she would do just fine.

But that was before the storm came up, and the moon disappeared, and the wind began to whip at her. Right now, every scary rumor seemed highly plausible and she was definitely looking over her shoulder for marauding royalty.

Earlier, when the sun was still shining, she'd thought it might be interesting to meet the prince.

"What's he like, really?" she'd asked Susa. "When he's not enticing young women into his bedroom, at any rate."

Susa shrugged. "I don't know much about him. Only that his young wife died years ago and he's been sort of a recluse ever since."

"Oh." Isabella thought she'd heard something about that a long time ago, but she didn't remember any details. "How sad."

"They say she died under mysterious circumstances," the woman added ominously.

"Are there any other kind in your world?" Isabella shot back.

Susa gave her a superior look and turned away, but at the same time Isabella was remembering what Noni Braccini, the restaurant cook who had taught her most of what she knew about Italian cooking when she was a young girl, used to say.

"Nothing good could happen in a place like that." She would point a wrinkled finger toward where the old, crumbling palazzo stood and mutter, "Bats."

Isabella would look at her, nonplussed. "Bats?"

She would nod wisely. "Bats. You don't want bats in your hair."

Isabella would find herself smoothing down her own wild tresses and agreeing quickly, with a shudder. "No, no, indeed. I don't want bats in my hair."

And that was about all she knew about the prince in the castle. Of course, there was the fact that the essential herb grew on a hillside on castle grounds.

Noni had died long since, but Susa was still around to give dire warnings, and she'd said matter-of-factly as Isabella was going out the door, "When I was a girl, it was common knowledge that the Rossi prince was a vampire."

"What?" Isabella had laughed aloud at that one. "Susa, that's crazy!"

"He was the grandfather of this one." The older woman had shrugged. "We'll see, won't we?"

Isabella had laughed all the way to her car, but she wasn't laughing now. It wasn't just what Susa had said in warning. There were plenty of other old stories swirling in her head. Her childhood had been full of them—tales told in the dark at girlfriend sleepovers, stories of blackbeards who captured women and held them within the castle walls—vampires who roamed the night looking for beautiful victims with virgin throats—seducers with dark, glittering eyes, who lured innocent girls into their sumptuous bedrooms. Suddenly they all seemed too plausible. She was half regretting that she'd come to this frightening place at all, and half angry with herself for being such a wimp.

"Come on," she muttered to herself encouragingly. "Just a bit further and we'll get this done."

After all, how bad could it be? Even if she did run into the prince, he couldn't possibly be as wicked as Susa had painted him. In fact, she remembered seeing him once, years ago, when she was a teenager. She'd been visiting a hot springs resort area a few hours from the village and someone had pointed him out. She'd thought him incredibly handsome at the time—and incredibly arrogant-looking.

"The old royalty are all like that," her friend had said. "They think they're better than the rest of us. It's best to stay out of their way."

And she had, all these years. Now she was rambling around on royal grounds. The quicker she got this over with, the better.

Just a little further and she would find the hillside where the special basil grew, pick enough to fill the canvas bag she'd brought along, and head for home. Of course, it would help if she could see more than three feet in front of her with this stupid flashlight that kept blinking off.

"Oh!"

Her foot slipped and she almost tumbled down the hill. At least the problem with the flashlight was solved. It *did* tumble down the hill, and over a ledge, and into the river. Even above the noise of the wind, she could hear the splash.

Isabella wasn't one to swear, but she was working up to it tonight. What a disaster. What had she been thinking when she'd decided to come here all alone in the middle of the night? She'd known she was just asking for trouble.

"I just wasn't made for this cloak-and-dagger stuff," she muttered to herself as she tried to climb higher on the hill. All she wanted was to find the herbs and get out of here. She hated doing this. She dreaded getting caught by guards…or the prince. Or attacked by vampires—whichever came first.

The wind slashed through the tops of the trees, howling like a banshee. Lightning flashed, and in that same moment she looked up and saw a figure all in black atop a huge horse, racing down on her.

Time stopped. Fear clutched at her heart like a vise. This was too much. The dark, the wind, the sight of danger crashing toward her—had she taken a wrong turn somewhere? Suddenly, everything was upside down and she was terrified. Without a pause, she screamed at the top of her lungs. The sounds echoed through the valley, louder and louder, as lightning cracked and thunder rolled.

That lifetime of scary stories had set her up to think the worst. Every story flashed through her soul in an instant. She was shaking now, panic taking over, and she turned to run.

She heard him shout. Her heart was in her throat. She was dashing off blindly, startled as a cornered deer, and she heard him coming up behind her. The hoofbeats sounded like thunder striking stone, and his shout was angry.

She was in big trouble. He was going to catch her. She couldn't let that happen! She had to run faster…faster…

She couldn't run fast enough and she couldn't get her breath. Her foot slipped, wrenching her balance out from under her. She started to slide down the steep hill. Crying out, she reached to catch herself on a bush, but it pulled right out of the ground. Suddenly, she was tumbling toward the river.

She hit the water with a splash that sent a spray in all directions. She gasped as the icy water took her in. Now she was going to drown!

But she barely had time to reach for the surface before the strong arms of the man in black had caught hold of her and she was pulled instantly from the racing water.

He had her. Stunned by the cold, shocked by what was happening, she couldn't find her bearings. Disoriented in the moment, she realized dimly that she was being carried toward the horse, but she was a bystander, watching helplessly, as though from afar. For now, it seemed there was nothing she could do to resist.

Later, she was mortified as she remembered this scene. How could she have succumbed so quickly to the overwhelming sense of his strength like that? She'd just suffered a shock, of course, and that had pretty much knocked her silly, but still... As she remembered just how much the feel of his strong, muscular arms seemed to paralyze her reactions, she could do nothing but groan aloud in frustration. How could she have been such a ninny?

But in the moment, she was spellbound. The moon came out from behind the clouds, turning the landscape silver. Trying to look up at his face, all she could see was his strong chin, and the smooth, tight cords of his sculptured neck. And still, she couldn't seem to make a move.

This was crazy. He was just a man. Nothing supernatural at all. Just a man. A man who had no right to carry her this way. She had to assert herself, had to let him know what he was dealing with. But before she could get a word out, she found herself thrown up onto the horse and the creature who'd captured her was rising to mount behind her.

And finally, with a lot of effort, she found her voice.

"Hey, wait a minute!" she cried. "You can't do this. Let me go!"

Maybe he didn't hear her. The wind was making a riot in the tops of the trees. At any rate, he didn't answer, and in seconds the horse was galloping toward the ancient, forbidding structure looming at the top of the hill, and she was going along for the ride. She hung on for dear life. She could hardly breathe. She heard the hoofs clattering on the cobblestones as they neared the entrance. Huge lanterns lit the entryway. And then they came to a halt and he had dismounted and pulled her down as well.

She swayed. For a moment, she was confused and couldn't find her footing. His hands gripped her shoulders from behind, holding her steady. She turned, wanting to see his face, but he kept it from her.

"This way," he said, taking her by the hand and leading her up to the huge wooden door.

"No," she said, but her voice was weak and she found herself following along where he led, even though her soggy running suit was sticking to her legs, the heavy jacket flapping against her torso, the running shoes sloshing with every step. She was a mess. She hated to think what her hair looked like.

Somewhere on the grounds, a pair of dogs began to howl. Or was it wolves? Her heart was thumping so hard she could hardly tell. The roll of distant thunder added to the menace in the air. The lanterns made eerie shadows and her gaze rose to take in the sinister spikes at the top of the castle wall.

She shuddered. Was she dreaming? Or had she ventured by mistake into one of this area's old-fashioned legends? Was she on her way to the dungeon, as Susa had warned?

And if this was a story, was this man who'd scared her and then saved her the hero or the villain?

"Both," said a little voice inside her.

She shook her head. It didn't matter right now. She needed him. She had no one else to turn to.

The front door creaked open as they approached. She caught a glimpse of a man as old and craggy as the walls, his features exaggerated by the lighting. A wizard? She shrank back against her companion, automatically turning to him for protection despite everything. He hesitated for a moment, then put his arm around her shoulders and let her curl herself up against him. After a second or two, his arm actually tightened around her.

Isabella was still too dazed to know what was really going on. She was wet, she was cold, she was in the courtyard of a forbidden palazzo, and a man she had momentarily thought might be a vampire—well, just for a second or two—now had his arm around her. What was more, his arm felt darn good, as did the rest of him. In fact, she didn't think she'd seen a man in a long time that appealed to her senses quite as much as this scary and yet comforting man did right now.

She'd pretty much decided men and romance and things of that nature weren't going to be a part of her life. Too much trouble, not worth the effort. And here she was, responding to this scary man like a cat to cream. Maybe she was just an adrenaline junky after all.

"We're almost there," he told her helpfully.

That surprised her. Were vampires usually this considerate? She didn't think so. But maybe he was just calming her fears to make her more amenable to manipulation. Or maybe she'd seen too many horror movies in her time.

She sighed and closed her eyes, wishing she could get

orientated. She wasn't used to feeling so helpless, as though her muscles couldn't really respond. But maybe that was because her mind didn't seem to be working at all. She was so tired. Maybe when she opened her eyes, this would all fade away and she would be home in her own bed....

Prince Maximilliano Di Rossi looked down at the woman who was clinging to him and frowned. He was surprised that she'd turned to him for protection the way she had, but he was also surprised at his own reaction to her move. His first impulse was to pull away, to reject all contact. That was his way, the style he'd been living with for the last ten years. The only people he allowed near him were those who had always been closest to him, a few people who had known him since childhood—since before the accident. He never had other visitors. He'd been stepping out of character even to bring her here.

But something in the easy, open way she'd clung to him had stirred old memories. She was shivering and turning toward him as a lover would. Something deep inside him hungered for this. It had been so long since he'd held a woman in his arms, since he'd felt that warmth, that contrast between his own hard body and the soft, rounded responsiveness of a woman. He'd thought he might never feel it again. And yet, here it was, like a gift out of the blue.

But not for long. He knew she'd been trying to see his face and he'd been keeping it averted. Once she really saw **him** in full light, any instincts for touching him in any way would dry up like summer rain on a hot pavement.

With a cynical twist of his wide mouth, he turned and led her into the palazzo through the tall, heavy wood door. Their footsteps echoed down the long empty hallways. Someone coughed. He looked up. There stood his man,

Renzo, in his nightclothes and dressing gown, and wearing what appeared to be a pair of aging woodchucks on his feet. He looked sleepy and ridiculous, but definitely alarmed at the same time.

"Nice slippers," he commented wryly, cocking an eyebrow.

"Thank you, sir," Renzo responded, shuffling his feet and looking slightly abashed.

Max paused for a moment. He knew he could very easily hand over this piece of womanly baggage to the individual who had been his combination valet, butler, and personal assistant most of his life. Hand her over and turn his back and walk away and never give her another thought. He knew very well that Renzo would take care of everything discreetly and efficiently. Doing just that would fit the pattern of his life, the way things were done around here. He made a move as though to do it. He could see that Renzo expected it. How easy it would be to follow through.

And then he glanced down at the woman. She was still turning to him for refuge. She'd reached for him, given herself into the comfort of his arm, pressed her beautiful young body against his as though she was trusting that he would keep her safe. Something moved inside him—and that was dangerous. Just looking down into her gorgeous thick, tangled hair, he could feel his emotions stirring in a way he didn't need.

And still, he didn't leave.

Later he told himself it was nothing more than a typical impulse of the male role of guardian, the same he might have had for a puppy or a kitten that needed his attention. Despite his background, despite his guilty past, the urge to safeguard those smaller and more vulnerable rose in him and he'd followed his instincts.

But for once, he wasn't convinced. No, there was something about this woman—something threatening. He knew he should walk away and leave her to Renzo to deal with.

But he didn't do that.

Looking up, he shook his head at his man. "I'll handle this," he said, shedding his long black cloak and dropping it on a chair along the side of the room. He was going to see to her himself.

At the same time he realized what this meant. He was going to be forced to go against habit and his recent tradition. He was going to have to do something he almost never did these days. He was going to have to turn and let her see his face.

Renzo looked alarmed. "But, sir—" he began.

The prince cut him off. "Notify Marcello that I would like him to join us in the Blue Room," he said.

Renzo blinked. "Excuse me, sir, but I think the doctor is asleep…"

"Then wake him," Max said crisply. "I want him to take a look at this young lady. She's had a fall."

"Oh, my goodness," Renzo said faintly, but he didn't leave the room. Instead, he cleared his throat as though to say more, but Max wasn't listening. He was steeling himself for the moment that was about to come.

He knew his hesitation would seem strange to others. Most would let anyone see their face at any time. After all, it was the side they showed to the world, the representation of just who they were.

But he wasn't like everyone else. His face was scarred, horribly damaged and ugly to see. It couldn't represent him, because he wasn't like that inside. But it was all he had, and therefore it was something he avoided showing to strangers.

To turn and let her see his face would be a serious step for him. Still, he was going to do it. He was impatient with himself for even wavering. It was time he got over this weakness. He would turn and let her see just what she was dealing with. And he would hold his gaze steady so that he would be forced to take in every ounce of the shock and horror in her eyes. It was best to stay real.

"Come this way," he told her brusquely, turning to stride down the hall. She almost ran to keep up, holding onto his hand as though she would be lost if she let go. The huge portraits that lined their path were a blur, as were the long, aging tapestries that hung from the walls. He swept her into a room lined with heavy blue velvet drapes. The embers of a dying fire were smoldering in the large stone fireplace.

"Sit down," he said, gesturing toward an antique Grecian couch. "My cousin Marcello is a physician. I want him to take a look at you."

"I can't," she said, shaking her head and looking down at herself. Everything about her seemed to be dripping. "I'm filthy and muddy and wet. I'll ruin the upholstery."

"That doesn't matter," he said shortly.

She raised her dark gaze and cocked her head to the side, trying to see more than the left half of his face. Was he joking? This was one of the most sumptuously embellished rooms she'd ever been in. Not what she was used to, but most people she knew didn't do much decorating in velvet and gold leaf.

"Of course it matters," she responded, beginning to feel some of her usual fire returning. "I may not look like much right now, but I've got manners. I know how to act in polite company."

"Polite company?" He gave a little grunt, not even sure himself if it were partly a laugh or not. "Is that what you're expecting? We'll have to see if we can muster some up for you."

He was pacing about the room in a restless way and she turned to keep him in her line of vision. She was pretty sure she knew who he was by now. After all, she'd seen him all those years ago at the hot springs. If only she could get a full view of his face she would know for sure, but he seemed to have a talent for keeping in the shadows.

"You're making me dizzy," she said, reaching out to steady herself with a hand on the back of an overstuffed chair.

He grunted again, but he didn't stop moving. She watched nervously, wondering what he was planning to do with her. Luckily, he didn't seem inclined to lock her in a cell, so Susa was wrong there, but she supposed he could call the police and have her arrested if he wanted to. This was his castle and she didn't belong here.

She watched and waited. She liked the way he moved. There was a controlled, animal strength to him, and every action, every turn, presented with a certain masculine grace. And yet there was the sense of something more to him, something hidden, something leashed and waiting. He was new to her, unpredictable. Once again she realized that she was in a presence she didn't know how to handle. That made her heart thump.

Stopping to look out into the hall, he muttered something she couldn't quite make out, but it sounded slightly obscene.

"What's the matter?" she asked, tensing as though to be ready to run for it.

He started to turn toward her, then stopped. "My cousin is taking his own sweet time about it," he said evenly. "I'd like to get this over with."

"So would I," she said, her tone heartfelt. "Listen, why don't I just go and—?"

"No," he ordered firmly, glancing at her sideways. "You stay right where you are."

That put her back up a bit and sparked a sense of rebellion in her soul.

"Much as I appreciate your warm and welcoming hospitality," she began with a touch of sarcasm, taking a step toward the door, "I think it's time—"

"No."

He took a step closer and his hand shot out and circled her wrist. "You're staying right here until I permit you to go."

"Oh, I am, am I?" Her lower lip jutted out and she pulled hard on his hold but he wasn't letting go. "Your rules are on the medieval side, you know. These days one doesn't take orders from another person unless they are being paid money."

He pulled her closer, his face half turned her way. "Is that what you're after?" he asked harshly. "Is it money you want?"

"What?" She stared up at him, shocked by the very concept. "No, no, of course not."

"Then what do you want here?" he demanded.

She swallowed hard. Somehow this didn't seem to be a good segue into asking for monthly access to his hillside. "N…nothing," she stammered.

"Liar."

She gasped. He was right but she didn't like hearing it. "You…you wouldn't understand," she stammered senselessly. "But I meant you no harm."

He gave a sharp tug to her wrist, pulling her up close. "Harm." He said it as though it were a pointless word. "All the harm's been done years ago," he added softly.

She winced at the bitterness in his voice. It was clear something about his life just wasn't going well. The gloomy, bleak atmosphere was only reinforced by his dark attitude.

Negative people usually turned her off but there was a lot more here than a bad mood. She felt it like a vibration in the air, and her heart began to beat just a bit harder.

He felt her pulse quicken under his hold on her wrist and he knew what he had to do. Slowly, very deliberately, he turned and faced her, the light from the lamps and the fire exposing his horrible scars.

Was it pride that kept him from showing this to anyone who didn't know him intimately? Was it conceit, arrogance, egoism? Was it really that hard to think that his face, which had once been considered quite handsome, was now so repellent, people turned away rather than be forced to look at him?

It was probably all those things. But he'd known from the start there was something deeper and harder to face than that. He knew very well there was a large measure of guilt mixed into his motivations. His scars were retribution for his sins, but, even more painful, they were his own fault. That was the hardest thing to live with.

He'd spent years now, hidden away, traveling in limousines with tinted windows, moving anonymously from one house to another. It was a strange, lonely existence, and he was sick of it. But in order to change things, he would have to get used to people seeing his face, and he wasn't sure he could do it. Or that he deserved to.

But tonight, he wasn't going to dodge anything. It was high time he accepted his fate and learned to live with it. He was going to stare directly into her huge blue eyes and read every scrap of emotion that was mirrored there. No more avoidance. His jaw tightened and he steeled himself. And then he presented himself to her, scars and all.

Her eyes widened as she took in the totality of his face. The shock was there. He tensed, waiting for the disgust, the wince, the hand to the mouth, the flood of pity, the eyes darting away, looking anywhere but at him. He'd seen it before.

The only mystery was—why did he still let it bother him? It was time to harden himself to it. And so he stood his ground and met her gaze.

But things weren't going quite as he'd expected. The quality of her surprise was somehow different from what he was used to. No curtain of instant distance appeared, no revulsion, no reserve tainted her manner.

Instead of dread, instead of a cold drawing away in repugnance, a warm, curious light came into her eyes. Rather than pull away, she was coming closer. He watched in astonishment as she actually cocked her head to the side, then reached out for him.

He didn't move as she edged closer and touched his face, her fingertips moving lightly over the scar, tracing its path down his cheek and into the corner of his wide mouth.

"Oh," she said, letting it out in a long sigh.

But there was no pity. Maybe there was a hint of sorrow. But other than that, only a touch of confusion along with much interest and curiosity. It seemed almost as though she'd found a wonderful piece of statuary with a tragic flaw that deserved a little exploring. And she felt no inhibitions in doing exactly that.

CHAPTER TWO

ISABELLA was moving in a haze of unreality, as though she really had stepped into a fairy tale. She saw the jagged, fascinating scars, the tragic flaw that split his face in two and made her heart ache with compassion, but there was so much beside that. There was power and presence in the man, and, even more, there was overwhelming beauty in him. His shirt was open, exposing the tanned skin of a hard, sculptured chest, and his wonderful male heat filled her with a strange sense of longing that scared her more than anything else had—and at the same time it tugged at her with an impossible attraction.

He reached out as though to steady her, his hands gentle yet firm on her shoulders, and she felt herself melt into his touch, wanted to lean closer yet. She had a sudden, wild desire to press her lips to the pulse she could see beating hard at the base of his throat. She stared at it, irresistibly drawn.

But she recoiled in time, shocked at her own impulses. What next—was she going to offer herself to the man outright? She gasped softly, then began to think she ought to pull away. Ought to—but couldn't quite summon up the will.

Max couldn't have been more amazed if she *had* kissed him. The moment crystallized in time, her body arched toward his, her fingertips on his face, his heart pounding, his gaze locked on hers. Something twisted in his chest and he realized he was holding his breath. He was feeling something new and strange and he didn't like it at all. But she'd touched him. No woman had done that since the accident. No woman had wanted to. That lit a fire inside him he hadn't known he was capable of feeling. Whatever else this young woman was, she was unique in a way he'd never seen before. She didn't make him feel like a freak. He savored the moment.

And in the same instant he became aware that Renzo had come into the room at last and was now lurching forward as though he was prepared to push this woman back away from his prince. It all seemed to be happening in slow motion. And it all seemed to be so very beside the point, but it had to be dealt with, and so he did.

Turning to block Renzo's ridiculous protective lunge with the position of his body, he pulled the young woman up against him and out of Renzo's reach. Looking down, he sank into the clouds in her dark eyes, searching for the mysteries they might contain. She seemed to hold worlds he'd never visited deep inside her. Those worlds were suddenly the most interesting places he'd ever had a glimpse of. He suddenly found it very hard to pull away from her gaze. Or maybe, the truth was, he didn't want to.

Who was she? Where had she come from? Should he get away from her as fast as he could—or should he find a way to keep her here? He knew what his instincts were telling him. But he knew from experience that his instincts could lie.

Renzo still hung at his shoulder. "Sir…"

It took Max a moment to respond. He was still looking deep into the young woman's eyes. "I thought I told you to get Marcello," he said without turning.

"But, sir…" Renzo was blinking rapidly, obviously upset by this strange behavior.

"Go."

Renzo averted his gaze, bowed deeply, and gave in. "Very well, sir." Turning on his heel, he left the room.

And at the same time Max's sister, Angela, appeared in the opening. She took in the scene and her eyebrows arched even higher than usual.

"Well, Max," she said, starting into the room at last. "Who's this?"

The sound of her voice snapped them both to attention as though a spell had been broken. They turned to look at her. She came closer, circling and gazing with wonder at the two of them.

"Where on earth did you find her?"

Max drew in a sharp breath and stepped away from Isabella as though she'd suddenly grown too hot to touch. She reached out to steady herself against the back of the couch, not sure if she was reacting to general dizziness, or to the man himself. She was still in a muddle, but at least her head was clear enough by now to fully understand whom she was dealing with. After all, if you trespassed on a prince's property, you were likely to run into the prince at some point. And maybe even a princess or two.

"I found her wandering around down by the river," this particular prince was saying. "The dogs were loose and I was afraid they might attack her." He made a gesture and looked down at Isabella, still swaying next to the couch, then back at his sister. "I must have startled her. She fell down the hill."

Angela nodded, looking her over, then glanced sharply at Max. "Right into the water, I see."

"Yes."

"And you…you rescued her?"

His hands curled around the back of a chair and gripped so hard his knuckles were white. "Yes, Angela. I rescued her." He turned to stare at his sister with a measure of hostility.

"I see." She stared back, but looked away first, looking Isabella over again. "That still doesn't tell me who she is."

He turned to look at her, too, his large dark eyes dispassionate. All sense of a special tension between them seemed to have melted away.

"True," Max agreed. "Nor what she was doing on the property." He hesitated, then added, almost to himself, "And so close to the river."

Isabella drew herself up. Now that she was coming back down to earth, she was getting tired of being treated like a rather stupid child and talked about as though it didn't matter if she understood or not. For one trembling moment, she'd actually thought she and this man had a special connection of sorts, something quick and searing that was going to change her life. But now she could see that she'd been fooling herself—as usual.

First he'd terrified her, then beguiled her with his tenderness and his scarred face. Now he was acting as if she were a wet cat who shouldn't have been let inside. The disappointment she felt was real. She noticed he was avoiding her gaze again, turning his head so that the scarred side was hidden by shadows. Her chin rose and she looked at them both defiantly, her pride returning.

"My name is Isabella Casali. I help my father Luca run the restaurant in the square. Rosa? Perhaps you've eaten there."

Angela gave a careless shrug. Dressed in a flowing robe, she'd obviously been preparing for bed when the sounds of Isabella's arrival had drawn her back downstairs. In her mid-thirties, she had a cool, blonde beauty that was slightly marred by just a touch too much arrogance for comfort.

"I know it though we've never eaten there." Her smile was perfunctory. "We will have to try your food someday."

Isabella was surprised. Everyone ate at Rosa. "You've never had anything from our restaurant?" Isabella asked, incredulous.

"No."

She looked from the handsome woman to the incredible man. Despite her newfound annoyance with him, she had to admit he was a striking figure with the sort of presence that demanded more than simple respect. Tall and muscular in a slender way that bespoke strength along with graceful movement, he was the sort of man you couldn't take your eyes off once you'd seen him. And that scar...she'd never seen anything like it before.

"Perhaps my aunt's restaurant, Sorella, is more to your liking," she commented. "She has things that are very international and trendy. It's right next door to Rosa."

He shook his head. "We have our own cooks," he said simply. "We don't eat in restaurants."

Her head went back. That certainly put her in her place.

"Oh," she said faintly. "Of course."

"I'm sure we can make an exception," Angela said with a wave of her hand, giving her brother a look as though to remind him to be polite to the little people. "To complete the introductions, this is Prince Maximilliano Di Rossi, who owns this palazzo, and I am his sister, Angela. If you live in Monta Correnti, I'm sure you know that."

Isabella didn't answer. It took a moment to get all this in focus. Of course, she'd known there was a Rossi prince living here in the castle from time to time, but, except for stories and the one sighting at the springs, she'd never actually given him much thought. He wasn't a regular presence in the village or around the countryside, so if she'd ever known his name, she'd forgotten it long since.

When she'd been young, there had been a Prince Bartholomew who had lived here. If she remembered correctly, he'd had a beautiful film-star wife who had seldom come here with him, and three teenaged children who had come occasionally. She'd seen them every now and then, but they were years older than she was and she hadn't paid much attention. The family hadn't mixed with their neighbors then, either, and no one knew much about them. The castle on the top of the steep hill was dark and imposing and pretty scary-looking, which was part of the reason legends about strange goings-on there were rife. People tended to give it a wide berth.

She thought now that Prince Bartholomew must have been this prince's father.

"And that brings us back to the question of why you were on the grounds," Max said coolly. "Since you live here in the area, I'm sure you understand that you were trespassing."

Isabella's chin rose again and she looked at him defiantly. "Yes, I know that."

He shrugged extravagantly, a clear response to her bravado. "And so…?" he asked, pinning her down with his direct gaze.

She drew her breath in sharply. She was caught, wasn't she? What could she do but tell him the truth?

That meant talking about the unique basil that grew on his hillside, and she really didn't want to do that. Very few people knew the identity of their special ingredient and they had kept it that way to discourage copycat trouble.

"If I could patent the *Monta Rosa Basil*, I would do so,"

her father was always muttering. "Just don't talk about it to others. We don't want anyone to know where we get it. If others started to use it, we would be in big trouble."

"No one else would make sauces as good as yours, even with the basil," Isabella would respond loyally.

"Bah," he would say. "It's our secret. Without it, we're doomed."

So she didn't want to tell the Rossi family what she'd come for. But now, she felt she had to. Besides, there was very little chance that they would care or tell other chefs anything about it. So she tried to explain. "I...I came because I had to. You see, there is a certain herb that only seems to grow on the southern-facing hill above your river." She shrugged, all innocence. At least, she hoped it was coming off that way. "I need it for our signature recipe at the restaurant."

"You *need* it?" Angela sniffed. "That's stealing, you know."

Isabella frowned. How could she explain to them that stealing from the prince's estate was considered a time-honored tradition in the village?

"I wouldn't call it that exactly," she hedged, but Max gave a cold laugh, dismissing her excuse out of hand.

"What would you call it, then?" he demanded.

She shrugged again, searching for a proper term. "Sharing?"

She looked at him hopefully. He looked right into her eyes and suddenly a hint of that connection that had sparked between them before was hovering there, just out of reach.

"Sharing?" he repeated softly.

She nodded, searching his eyes for signs that the coldness in his gaze might melt if she said the right things, but there wasn't much there to give her hope.

"Doesn't that require the consent of those 'shared' with?"

"I...well, you could give your consent," she suggested. "If only you would." She was still held by those huge dark eyes. Her heart was beating quickly again, as though something were happening here. But nothing was. No, she was sure of it. Nothing at all.

"Never," he said flatly, his gaze as cool as ever. "Never," he said more softly. "The river is too dangerous."

She stared up at him, captivated by the impression of energy she sensed from him. It felt as though he had a certain sort of power trapped and controlled inside him, just waiting for a release. What would it take to free him? Could she do it? Did she dare try?

When Angela's voice, saying goodnight, snapped her out of her reverie again, she had to shake herself and wonder just how long it had lasted. For some reason, she felt almost as though she knew him now. Almost as though they had always known each other. Not friends, exactly. Maybe lovers? Her breath caught in her throat at that brazen thought.

But Max was hardly thinking along those lines himself. He obviously wanted to get on with it. "If you'll just take a seat," he began impatiently, but his sister, halfway out of the room, turned back and let out a rude exclamation.

"She's soggy," she stated flatly.

Exactly what Isabella had said herself, but somehow the way this woman said it carried a bit of a sting. She bit her lip. Why was she letting these people play with her emotions like this? She was out of place here, in way above her head. She needed to leave. Quickly, she spun on her heel and started for the door.

"I'll just get out of your way," she snapped, glancing at the prince as she tried to pass him. "I should be getting home anyway..."

His hand shot out and curled around her upper arm. "Not until Marcello takes a look," he said, pulling her a bit too close. She gasped softly, then shook her head, ready to object. But the prince's sister beat her to the punch.

"As you can see, her condition is unacceptable," Angela said briskly. "We need to get her cleaned up before she sees Marcello." She made a face in her brother's direction. "It will only take a moment. I'll run her under a quick shower and have her back here in no time."

She gestured toward Isabella as she might have toward a servant. "Come along with me," she ordered.

Rebellion rose in Isabella's throat. She was beginning to feel like Eliza Doolittle in *My Fair Lady*. Shades of the little peasant girl being cleaned up and prepared to meet with her betters. No, thanks. She didn't really care for that role. It didn't suit her. She'd considered the options and decided against it.

She was regaining her bearings and beginning to feel a bit foolish. She'd been caught red-handed, so to speak, and deserved to get a little guff for it. But this was getting out of hand. After all, if the man didn't want her on his property, why didn't he just let her go? Why had he forced her to come back here to the house? She was certainly in a wet, bedraggled condition, but still…

"Why don't I just go?" she began, turning toward the door again.

"You have no choice in the matter," the prince said calmly. "For the good of all, you need to be clean and dry."

"But—"

"Go with my sister," the prince said. His voice was low and composed, but something in it made Isabella look up, surprised at how coolly he could give an order that made you want to do exactly what he said. "You fell on our land, into our river. We are responsible for your condition. It's only right that we make you whole again."

That didn't make any sense at all. She'd been trespassing, not visiting. But somehow she found herself following Angela down the hall. She looked back. The prince was watching her go, half leaning against the couch, his head lowered. For some crazy reason, that made her heart lurch in her chest. She turned away quickly and followed where Angela led, but the shivers his look had given her lingered on.

Max stayed where he was, listening as their footsteps faded down the hall, staring into the darkness where she'd just been. He was drawn to her and he hadn't been attracted to a woman for a long, long time. A picture of his beautiful wife, Laura, swam into his head and he closed his eyes as though to capture it there. Instead, it melted away and another face drifted into its place.

His eyes snapped open and he swore softly. This girl, this Isabella, was nothing like Laura. Why would he see her in his mind's eye? It was ridiculous to even begin comparing them. She was just a girl from the village. She meant nothing to him and never could.

Slowly, his hand rose until he touched the scar on his face. He wanted to feel what she had felt with her fingertips. What an odd young woman. Oddly compelling. Her reaction had been different from that of anyone he'd ever met and it still puzzled and intrigued him. Had she seen something no one else had? What had she found that had interested her that way? Had anything changed while he hadn't been paying attention?

No. Same old face. Same old scars. Cursing softly, he jerked his hand away and turned toward the fire. For a moment, he almost hated her.

And why not? She represented the world he'd given up almost ten years ago, the world he had to deny himself. He'd done a damn good job of keeping that world at bay. Now it seemed to have come looking for him. For his own sanity, he knew he had to resist its temptations. This dark, gloomy palazzo was his reality. There was no other way.

Isabella looked around her as she emerged from the steamy shower. It was an antiquated room with antiquated plumbing, but luxurious in an old-fashioned way, with high ceilings and a huge claw-footed tub in the middle of the room. She dried quickly and then stepped before a full-length mirror to check herself for damage.

What she saw made her gasp, then laugh softly. The area around her right eye was looking as if she'd smudged it with soot. A black eye! How was she going to explain that to her customers? She groaned, then began to check out the rest of her body. There was a large painful bruise on her hip and a rather deep cut on her right leg, just below the knee. Most of the blood had been soaked up by her running pants, but there was still some seeping out. Other than a few places that felt a bit achy, that seemed to be it.

Turning, she looked at the clothes Angela had set out for her—a lacy cream-colored sweater and tan stretch pants. They were very close to things she might have picked for herself, so she put them on without hesitation, covering her still bleeding wound with a wad of tissue.

"Are you decent?" Angela called as she was combing and fluffing her hair. She came in after Isabella invited her, handing her a bag with her wet clothes.

"Here you go. Marcello ought to be with Max by now. They'll be waiting in the Blue Room." She yawned. "I'm going back to bed. Goodnight, my dear."

"Wait." Isabella turned and hesitated, then went ahead and asked, "What happened to his face?"

Angela stared at her for a long moment before answering. "There was a terrible car accident. It was almost ten years ago, the same night that…" She stopped herself and shook her head. "It was a very bad accident. For days, we were sure that he would die."

Isabella frowned, taking that in. She had a feeling there was more to it than that. There was a weird, moody undercurrent to everything that went on here. She wanted to know more, but she could hardly ask many questions now.

"But he survived."

"Obviously. But his face…" Throwing out her hands, she turned away. "He was quite handsome, you know," she said softly.

Isabella shrugged. "He still is."

She turned to stare at Isabella. "You think so, do you?"

"Oh, yes."

Her eyebrows rose. "Well…" she said significantly. But she made a face and turned away. "Goodnight again, Isabella," she said, beginning to bustle out again. "I'm sure Max will make sure you get taken home safely once Marcello has given you his stamp of approval."

That sense of rebellion rose in her again, but Isabella thanked Angela as she left the room, then finished up making herself presentable. And all the while she was wondering how she could get out of this ancient stone building without running the gauntlet of the prince and his cousin. She was fine. She didn't need the attention of a doctor. And she especially didn't need to run into the prince again.

What she did need was the delicate and very special herb she'd come for. But she had to be realistic. Tonight was not her night. She would have to come back another time. Still, was that going to be possible? Now that she knew about the dogs…

Never mind. She would think about that later. Right now, she just needed to get out of here without seeing the prince again. She took one last look in the mirror. Her black eye was getting worse by the minute. In fact, half her face was now somewhat red and a bit swollen. She groaned. How was she going to hide this from the world?

And then it came to her—she was getting a small hint of what it must be like to be the prince with his vivid scar. She sighed softly as she thought of it. At least she knew that she would be healing soon.

Staring at her own face, she thought of how she'd touched him, and she gasped at her own reckless audacity. What on earth had possessed her to do a thing like that? And why had he stood for it? She must have still been groggy from the effects of the dunking she'd taken and the wild ride through the night on horseback. It really wasn't her habit to go poking at people's faces like that.

What had Susa said about him? That his wife had died, that he'd been something of a recluse ever since. Maybe that explained his cool, brooding manner. She shook her head and turned away. This was certainly a strange night and she was finding herself doing all sorts of strange things she'd never done before. It was time she got out of here.

Grabbing the bag with her clothes, she made her way quietly into the hall. She knew which way to turn for the Blue Room, so she took the other path, moving quickly to get away from where she might be seen.

Another sharp turn down a darker hallway and she found herself in the huge, cavernous kitchen. A night-light glowed at the end of the room, giving her just enough light to find her way. She stopped a moment, turning and admiring all

the pans and cooking equipment hanging from hooks along the walls. Just the sheer size of the place was impressive. It was three or four times as big as her kitchen at the restaurant. What she could do with a situation like this!

But she didn't have time for dallying, so she took it all in with one sweeping glance, then picked a door that looked as if it might head outside. She pulled it open quickly, stepped through and suddenly she was falling again—right into the arms of the prince.

CHAPTER THREE

ISABELLA screamed. Screaming was getting to be a habit, it seemed. She didn't think she'd screamed this much at any time in her life before. But she couldn't help it. Running into this strong, scary man in the dark just sent her over the top every time.

He held her for barely a second before she jumped back away from him. Still, at the same time she was recoiling and cursing her own continuing bad luck a traitorous part of her was entertaining the temptation to let herself relax in his arms again, to press her cheek against his chest and listen for his heartbeat. The moon was out again, sending beams in through a window just over their heads. What could be more romantic than to wrap herself in his arms and…?

Fanciful nonsense, of course. None of that could happen or would happen. She hadn't had such silly daydreams since she'd been a preteen and had been mooning after a boy named Romano Puccini. Bad things usually followed when you let your emotions run away with you. At least, that had been the lesson she had learned that long-ago summer.

"That's the second time tonight you scared me out of my wits," she told him accusingly.

"And that's the second time tonight I found you sneaking around where you shouldn't be," he shot back at her.

She tossed her hair, hooking the mop of it behind her ear with one quick swipe of her hand. "That's only true if you are the one who gets to set the rules of where I may or may not go."

He moved closer. Even in the dark, she could see the outline of his scar clearly. It was a slash of silver across his moonlit face. Eerie…otherworldly…and somehow alluring.

"And why wouldn't I set the rules?" he said firmly. "It's my house, remember?"

She looked up into his eyes. They seemed to glow in the dim light. "But you forget—I'm only passing through."

"Trespassing through, you mean."

Well, she had to give him that one. Suddenly she was so very tired.

"You know, I…I just want to go home." There was a quaver in her voice that she regretted, but, still, it was only the truth.

He took her hand, still looking down into what he could see of her face. "We all want things we can't have."

The hint of desolation in his voice hit her hard and stopped her from taking offense. An unexpected wave of sadness swept over her. She wanted to reach for him, to help him somehow. But then she remembered—he was the prince. What in the world could she do to comfort a man like this?

"Come back to the Blue Room and let Marcello take a look at you," he ordered, beginning to lead her that way. "After all this, we might as well go through with it." He glanced down at her as she walked beside him. "Then I'll have someone drive you home."

She sighed. She hated to admit how tempting it seemed to just follow wherever he led. She was going to have to

work on that. A little strength of character—a little more confidence in her own strength—that was what she needed.

"My car is…is down by the south wall." She flushed as she said the words. Oh, how guilty she sounded.

When he replied, he sounded bemused, but satirical. "So you drove yourself out from the village, parked along the wall, and then what? Did you vault over?"

"Not quite." She hesitated, but she didn't want to tell him that she'd sneaked in exactly where her father had been sneaking in for years. Only her father had the good sense to do it in daylight, and he'd never been caught.

"Not going to say, are you?" he said, sounding cynical again, as though he really did consider her an outlaw in his world. "You're going to keep it a secret. That way you can keep your options open for sneaking in again." He tugged on her hand, leading her around a sharp corner. "But I would advise against that, Isabella Casali. I think we'll have to let the dogs patrol twenty-four hours a day from now on." He glanced back at her. "I don't want you anywhere near that river."

That surprised her. She would have expected him to say he didn't want to risk any more interruptions to his own life and peaceful existence, not to her welfare. But maybe she was taking his words too kindly. Of course, that was exactly what he meant. After all, if she got hurt, he would have to deal with it. Still, there was something in his tone when he mentioned the river that gave her pause.

He stopped just outside the door to the Blue Room and stared down at her. For the first time the light was good enough for him to see what had happened to her face.

"My God! *Maledizione!*" His hands cupped her face, tilting it up so that he could see it fully. "You seemed a little bruised before, but this…"

"It's okay," she said, gazing up at him in wonder. He was so close. The sense of his male presence overwhelmed her. For a few seconds, she felt a wave of emotion sweeping away her common sense, and suddenly she wanted his kiss more than she'd ever wanted anything else in her life.

And that in itself was like a splash of cold water on her face. What was she thinking? She wanted to turn away so that he wouldn't read her guilty secret in her eyes, but he was staring so hard, from so close.

"I…I'm okay."

"It's hard to see something so fresh and lovely marred this way," he said as though it really did pain him. His voice was cool and it was evident that this was a philosophical problem and nothing to do with him personally. But at the same time his gaze ranged over her face as though he were memorizing every line, every dimple. "You're just so… so…" His voice faded without saying the word, whatever it was meant to be.

And then he kissed her. Like a moth to the flame, he couldn't stay away. It was a light kiss, barely a touching of his lips to her forehead, right above her blackened eye. She gasped as she felt him, but at the same time she knew he'd done it in a strange way as though to erase the damage, make it go away. He seemed to have an obsession with avoiding harm. That had to be it. It didn't feel personal. His gaze still looked as hard and cold, his bearing was still just as arrogant.

But still—he kissed her.

"Is this going to take much longer?" said the deep, masculine voice of a tall man standing in the doorway, cutting into the magic of the moment. "Because I could go back to my room and get a few winks in and you could call me down later."

Isabella gulped in dismay, but the prince only straightened, giving his cousin a brief look of outraged dignity. It was obvious their relationship was maintained with a closeness that was disguised by a lot of good-natured mockery.

"Isabella, this is Marcello Martelli, my cousin."

"I'm pleased to meet you, Isabella," Marcello said, shaking her hand briskly. "This shouldn't take too long, nor be too painful."

Marcello was young and very handsome. In fact he looked very much like what she assumed Max would look like without the scar. She couldn't help but give him a big smile in answer to his friendly greeting. Here he was, barefoot and in jeans and a T-shirt—looking for all the world like any of the young men she knew in the village would look if you knocked on their door after midnight. He had the ruffled hair and the sleepy eyes as well.

"You fell into the river, I hear," he said, leading her in to sit on the antique couch. His gaze flickered back and forth between her and Max as though he didn't completely buy it.

"Yes," she told him earnestly.

"But luckily Max came along in time to…to rescue you."

She turned and looked at where the prince was standing back in the shadows just in time to see him turn away as though angry at what his cousin had just said. She frowned. Why would he do that? Did he realize what a part he'd played in creating her unfortunate incident? Maybe he needed a reminder.

"Is that the way he tells the story?"

Marcello grinned at her. "How do you tell it?"

She gave Max an arch look sideways. "Here's how I remember it. I was strolling along on the hillside when suddenly something that looked like a dark avenging angel

came galloping down on me and I ran for my life. My foot slipped. I tumbled into the river." She shrugged. "A simple tale, really," she said.

"And all Max's fault," Marcello said with a knowing look.

Her eyes widened in mock innocence. "Of course." She glanced back at where Max was pacing, but she couldn't see his face.

"Here's what I don't quite get," Marcello was saying as he looked through his black bag for supplies. "What was it about Max that terrified you enough to start running?" He looked up at her. "Instead of just holding your ground and stating your case, I mean." He gave his cousin a mocking look. "He doesn't seem all that scary to me."

Yes, that was the slightly embarrassing element in all this, she had to admit. Should she tell him the truth? Would he laugh? Or think her a little looney? She glanced at Max again and his haughty reserve gave her the spark she needed to go on.

"I'm sure you know about the legends attached to this castle," she said. "I've heard them all my life."

Max stopped, though still in shadows. "What sort of legends?" he asked gruffly.

She hesitated, knowing he was going to scoff. "Well, the usual," she began, starting to wish she hadn't brought it up.

"I know what she's talking about," Marcello offered. "Village people love to think of their local prince as a modern day Casanova, seducing women and humiliating men." He gave his cousin a quick grin. "And you've got to admit we've got a few rakes and degenerates in the older branches of our family tree."

Max shrugged and turned away, and Isabella bit her lip, then added something in a very soft voice.

"Vampires," she said.

They both turned back to her. "What?"

Her chin came up and her eyes sparked. "Vampires," she said more forcefully.

They gaped at her and she went on quickly, before they could begin to laugh.

"There are plenty of rumors that your family has included vampires. I know it's crazy. I'm just saying…"

Max turned away again, shaking his head.

"It was partly the way you came crashing at me in the middle of a storm," she continued, raising her voice so that he couldn't ignore her. "Like something dropped from a thundercloud. And on horseback!" She shook her head. "I thought…I thought…" She bit her lip and wondered if she really should tell them this.

"Yes?" Marcello leaned forward, unmistakably interested. "What was it you thought?"

She narrowed her gaze and put steel in her spine. "I…I thought Max was a vampire. Just for a second or two."

There. She'd said it. She looked up at where Max was standing and wished she could see what his eyes were revealing at this very moment. It was difficult to tell his reactions and that was driving her crazy.

"Are you serious?" Marcello was another matter. His response was no mystery. "A vampire?"

She tossed her hair back and tried to explain, addressing Max directly, even if he wouldn't do the same to her.

"Well, it was a logical conclusion to draw. After all, you came galloping out of the forest, dressed all in black with that cape and everything. The setting was perfect for it with the moon hidden behind clouds over your shoulder. From where I was standing, it was like something right out of a vampire movie."

Max didn't move.

Marcello's mouth was holding steady but his gaze was rife with amusement.

"Isabella, I think you've got it wrong," he said carefully, as though teaching a lesson. "This is the Italian countryside, you know. As I understand it, vampires live in Transylvania. Am I right?"

Of course he was right, but she wasn't going to admit it so easily. "Oh, so you think an Italian can't be a vampire?" she demanded.

He shrugged grandly and almost rolled his eyes. "What do you think, Max? I'd say chances are slim."

Max didn't answer, but she wasn't giving up. She shook her head and threw out her arms. "They say there are vampires everywhere."

"I see." Marcello was laughing at her again. "How many have you met yourself?"

She gave him a quick, sideways look. "Well…not many, I will admit."

He nodded wisely. "Interesting."

His attitude was really beginning to annoy her, but even worse was the way the prince stayed silent through it all. She wanted some reply, some indication as to how he felt about the things she was saying, and she was getting nothing at all.

"So you actually haven't had a lot of experience with vampires."

"Max is the only one so far," she said tartly.

And that got the reaction she was after. Max swung around and came in front of her very much like the man who had swooped down upon her on horseback, bringing with him all the sense of power he seemed to carry with him, very much like that cape he'd worn.

"Miss Casali," he said icily, staring down at her, his full

scars exposed. "I may be many things, but I am not now, nor have I ever been, a vampire. If I start feeling a sudden craving for human blood, you'll be the first to know. Until then, drop this nonsense."

She swallowed hard, looking up at him. "Okay," she said in a small, soft voice. His gaze held hers for only seconds, but it made its mark. She felt as though she'd just had a wild ride on a roller coaster and her insides were still in flight.

"Marcello?" he said pointedly, then turned back to pace the shadows.

His cousin moved in to start his examination of the patient and, for now, all bantering ceased. He started with a look at her black eye, and what he saw had him shaking his head in dismay. "Ice will help the swelling," he told her after he'd checked to make sure there were no cuts or outright abrasions involved. "But the bruising will seem to go on forever. And there's really not much you can do about that."

There wasn't much he could do about her bruised hip, either. He tested her reactions and pronounced nothing broken. But the cut on her leg was deep and he decided a few stitches were in order.

She sat back obediently and didn't talk back. Her mind was swirling with emotions and reactions to the prince and to his fascinating life and home. What was she doing here? It was more than obvious she didn't belong. But she wouldn't have given up this chance at a taste of another sort of world for anything.

Max paced, then slumped into a chair and watched, feeling restless. He was torn. He wanted her out of here as quickly as possible. She disturbed everything about his life. And at the same time, he couldn't take his eyes off her. She was bad

news, but it was a sort of bad news it seemed he hungered for. Having her here made him remember the old days, when Laura was still alive and they traveled and held parties on the terrace and lived the life of international socialites, attending shows and meeting famous people and competing in yacht races and attending fabulous dinners in exotic locations. Their life together had only lasted a year and a half, but it had been an enchanted existence, a life of pleasure and comfort such as most people could only dream of.

It seemed almost too indulgent now, as he looked back on it. Maybe that had been the problem. Maybe they had taken things too much for granted. Maybe they had been too happy. Sometimes it seemed the fates wouldn't allow too much happiness.

Isabella laughed at something his cousin said and he frowned, holding back the curt comment that came to mind. He seemed to remember a time when he might have been as good at the give and take as Marcello was now. But that time was gone. He didn't expect he would ever get it back. Still, it was interesting to watch this playing out before him. It was so unusual to have a stranger among them.

She'd dropped into his world out of nowhere and she would soon go back to whence she came. But she was an anomaly and, with her bruised and swollen face, he almost felt as though they had something in common. That was ridiculous and he knew it. He was alone in his own private hell and no one else could understand what this was like. It would be best to get rid of her as quickly as possible.

Isabella knew he was watching her and his interest sparked a warm fire in her chest, a fire that was spreading and beginning to create such heat it scared her. It wasn't that she was unused to male attention. She'd had that all her life.

She was a beautiful woman, her features wide and sensual. She knew some men considered her extremely sexy. She'd never understood that. She didn't feel very sexy. Most of the time she just felt as though she had too much to do and too little time to do it in. Men just sort of got in the way.

But men liked her. Still, she had a sharp tongue at times and didn't suffer fools gladly, or any other way. Over the years, there had been very few men she'd thought were worth the effort.

Just recently her friend Gino had railed at her, accusing her of being cold and heartless. That had cut her to the core. He'd asked her to go with him on a weekend trip to Rome and she'd turned him down. In his disappointment, he'd charged her with living for her own immediate family and no one else.

"All you want to do is run this restaurant and make your father happy. You'll never have children. You'll be content to be an old maid, clucking like an old hen over your aging chicks, those worthless brothers and your old, sick father."

She could dismiss Gino with no effort at all, but his words didn't fade away quite so easily. The things he'd said echoed in her mind all the time lately. Was it true? Was she really so wrapped up in her little family that she'd lost the knack of feeling like a desirable woman? Would she never have room for a man in her life? What if he was right? What if there was something wrong with her?

But the things she'd been through tonight were relieving some of those doubts. She was all right. She could relate to men, on the level of friendship at the very least. Marcello obviously liked her and they got along famously.

And Max... He'd kissed her, hadn't he? It had been a light, gentle gesture of healing, but still... A kiss was a kiss. Even in her ugly, bruised condition, he'd felt a pull in her direction. And she'd felt it too.

And that was just the problem. She couldn't remember when she'd felt such a thrill at a man's touch. It had been years. But was there any promise there? Of course not.

Come on, Isabella, she chided herself a bit sadly. *He's a prince. You work in a restaurant. So what if there seems to be a sensual connection that flares between the two of you every time your eyes meet? He may find you amusing for the moment—though evidence of that is pretty skimpy— but there is no way anything real can happen between the two of you. So you might as well forget it.*

Marcello finished up giving her stitches and began to pack his equipment away in his little black doctor bag. He and Max talked back and forth for a moment, and then the prince said something that chilled her.

"We're going to have to beef up security around here," he was saying, not even looking her way. "I don't want anyone near the river."

She turned to look at him. Whenever the river was brought up, there was some undercurrent of emotion that she couldn't quite pin down. What was it about the river that had so spooked this family?

"The dogs don't do the trick?" Marcello said.

Max shrugged. "The dogs can't be everywhere all the time. And they have to sleep. They're dogs."

Marcello grinned. "That they are. Have you thought of hiring guards?"

"No." He flashed a warning look at his cousin. "You know I can't do that."

Marcello shrugged with resignation. "Of course."

"We'll put in an alarm service, with cameras. We'll get state-of-the-art security going around here. No one will be able to slip through the cracks again." He shrugged. "We should have done it long ago."

Isabella sighed. That meant she wouldn't get a second chance. What was she going to do? Hire James Bond? It didn't seem likely.

Marcello headed back to his room to get some sleep. Isabella felt a flutter of nerves at being alone with Max again, but he treated her with distant politeness, making her sit closer to the fire to dry her hair while he dispatched poor Renzo off to get her car and bring it up for her. And then he began to pace the room again, staying as far away from her as he could manage.

Her conversational gambits seemed to have dried up with Marcello out of the room. She fluffed her hair in the warmth of the fire and racked her brain for a subject as the silence between the two of them got louder.

"I like your cousin," she said at last, risking a quick look his way. "And I appreciate the medical attention." She threw him a quick smile and made an attempt at a light joke. "You treat trespassers well around here."

He gave her a piercing look, then turned back to stare into the fire. She noted he was getting less and less protective of the right side of his face. Did that mean he was getting less self-conscious? Or that he cared less what she thought?

"Yes," he said at last, speaking slowly. "Marcello is my friend as well as my cousin." He glanced her way. "He and I once looked very much alike," he added softly, almost as though musing to himself. "People took us for brothers."

She nodded. She could tell that, despite the scar. "He's very handsome," she said before she thought, then colored slightly as she realized how he might take that.

He glanced at her, eyebrow raised, but didn't say anything. She didn't speak again right away. She wanted to. She wanted to tell him his own face was so much more interesting than his cousin's. It had all the beauty Marcello

had, but it had something more—character, history, a hard and cruel story to tell. Just what that story was, she didn't know, but there was passion there, and mystery, and heart-break. It was a face for the ages, a map of human tragedy, a work of art.

The more she thought about it, the more she realized she preferred it. In fact, she found it beautiful in a rare and special way. But she couldn't say those things—could she? He would think she was flattering him, perhaps even trying to get something from him.

"You are both very handsome," she said at last, feeling a bit brave to say that much.

He shrugged, looking away. "My face is what it is. It is what I made it. My burden to bear."

She sat back, biting her tongue and wondering if she dared say any of the things she was thinking. He was wonderful to look at. Didn't he realize that?

Or was it her? Was she strange?

That was a loaded question and she didn't want to answer it. But she had to say something.

"You know what I think?" she began. "I think you should come to my restaurant. You need to get out and…"

He swore softly but it was enough to stop the words in her throat. "You don't know what you're talking about," he told her roughly. "You don't have a clue."

Of course she didn't. She knew that. But he didn't have to be so rude. She was only trying to help.

She bit her lip, considering the situation. For some reason, when he ordered her about, she often found herself wanting to do what he said. It was time to nip that in the bud. He was beginning to think of her as a pushover, wasn't he? Sure, he was a prince and she was a nobody—but that didn't matter. She'd never been the amenable one in any

relationship. Why let it get started now? She had to fight this drift toward subservience. Rising from her seat on the couch, she faced him with her hands on her hips, her head cocked at a challenging angle.

"I thought I should let you know that I don't really think you're a vampire," she said as an opening.

He nodded, looking at her coolly. "I was pretty sure about that all along."

"But you do have cruel tendencies," she said, looking at him earnestly. "Listen, about the herbs I need from your hillside—"

"No." He said it with utter finality.

She pulled her head back, startled by his vehemence. "But…"

He held a hand up to stop her in her tracks. "If keeping you off a dangerous hillside is cruel, I'm a monster. Sorry, but that is the way it is."

"But—"

"No. You're to stay away. And that's final."

He rose as if to add emphasis to his words. She looked up at him and swallowed hard. He looked tall and stern and unyielding, and his shoulders were wide as the horizon. There was no humor in his face, no softness at all. His scars were vivid and his hard eyes made the breath catch in her throat and her heart beat just a little faster. Just that quickly she was back to being a timid petitioner, and he was once again a prince. His gaze met hers and held. She couldn't say a thing.

And then, breaking the spell, Renzo appeared.

"The young lady's car is here, sir."

The prince turned and nodded.

"Thank you, Renzo."

It was very late. The grandfather clock in the hallway

was chiming the hour. A part of him wanted to accompany her down to her home. Gallantry would suggest it. But practicalities, as well as common sense, forbade it. Not to mention the fact that he just plain couldn't do it. So he merely nodded to her, staying back away so that he wouldn't be tempted to repeat anything as silly as a kiss.

"Renzo will show you to your car," he said shortly. "Goodnight." She opened her mouth to say something, but there was no time. Turning on his heel, he went back into his dark and lonely palazzo, leaving her behind as though that was the main purpose. She sighed, feeling suddenly cold and lonely. Renzo showed her to her car and she drove off toward her home and restaurant in the village with a sense of frustration. But she knew very well that her life had been changed…changed forever, even if she never saw him again.

CHAPTER FOUR

"WELL," Susa said the next morning as she began to mix the dough for the large cake pans that sat waiting. "How's the prince?"

Isabella turned bright red and had to pretend to be looking for something in the huge wall refrigerator in order to hide that fact until things cooled.

"What prince?" she chirped, biding her time.

Susa's laugh sounded more like a cackle. "The one who punched you in the eye," she said, elbow-deep in flour. "Don't say I didn't warn you."

Isabella whirled and faced the older woman, wondering why she'd never noticed before how annoying she could be. "No one punched me. I...I fell."

"Ah." Susa nodded wisely, a mischievous gleam in her gray eyes. "So he pushed you, did he?"

"No!"

Isabella groaned with exasperation and escaped into the pantry to assemble the ingredients for the basic tomato sauce that was the foundation of all the Casali family cuisine. Let Susa cackle if she felt like it. Isabella wasn't going to tell her anything at all about what had happened. Pressing her lips together firmly, she set about making the

sauce and pretended she didn't know what the older woman was talking about.

She couldn't discuss it yet. Not with anyone. She wasn't even sure herself what exactly had happened. Looking back, it seemed like a dream. When she tried to remember what she'd said or what he'd done, it didn't seem real. So she washed the clothes the prince's sister had loaned her, sent them back to the palazzo, and heard nothing in return. She had to put it behind her.

Besides, she had other problems, big problems, to deal with. She'd been putting off thinking about them because she'd assumed she would go to collect the *Monta Rosa Basil* and all would be well—or at least in abeyance. Without the basil, she was finally facing the fact that the restaurant was in big trouble.

Luca, her father and founder of Rosa, had gone into a panic when she had told him a sketchy version of what had happened and then tentatively speculated what life—and the menu—might be like without the herb.

"What are you talking about?" he demanded, looking a bit wild. A tall, rather elegant-looking man, in Isabella's eyes, he radiated integrity. Despite the demands he tended to put on her, she loved him to pieces.

"The old prince said I could come any time."

That was news to Isabella. She'd had no idea there was any sort of permission granted, and she had to wonder if it wasn't just a convenient memory her father had embellished a bit.

"Well, the new prince says 'no'."

"The new prince?" He stared at her. "You've talked to him?"

"Yes. A little."

He frowned. "No, Isabella. Stay away from the royalty.

It's no good to mix with them. They think they can walk all over us and they do it every time."

"But, Papa, if I'm going to try to get permission to—"

"You don't need permission."

She sighed. There was no way she was going to make him understand that the circumstances had changed.

"I'll go myself," he muttered. He tried to rise from his chair and she hurried to coax him back down.

"Father, you will not go anywhere," she said fretfully.

"Don't you understand how important this is? The *Basil* is our family's trademark, our sign of distinction. Without it we are just like all the others, not special at all. It's who we are, the heart and soul of our cuisine and of our identity. We have to have it."

She was feeling even worse about this than before. "But, Papa, if I can't get it any longer…"

He shook his head, unable to understand what the difficulty was. "But you can get it. Of course you can." His tired blue eyes searched hers. "I've never had any trouble. I go in right at sunrise. I go quietly, squeezing through the chink in the wall, right where I've entered the grounds since I was a young man. A short hike past the river and up the hill, and there it is, green leaves waving in the breeze, reaching up to kiss the morning sun." He kissed his fingertips in a salute to the wonderful plants that were the making of his reputation.

Then he frowned at her fiercely. "If you can't manage to do such a simple thing, I'll do it myself, even if I have to crawl up that hill. I've never failed yet."

That was it. She was a failure. She sighed. "The dogs never came after you?" she asked him, feeling almost wistful about it.

"The dogs are only out at night."

"Not anymore," she said sadly.

She left him pounding his walking stick on the tile floor and grumbling about incompetence, knowing she couldn't let him attempt the task. The climb up the hill would kill him in his current condition. She had to find a way.

Everyone knew there was a problem. The situation was getting desperate. Her father had let things go too long. They were losing customers and had been bleeding money even before this latest problem. To make matters worse, there was some nonsense about a permit her father had never bothered to get. Fredo Cavelli, an old friend of her father's and now on the local planning commission, had come by a few times, threatening dire consequences if the paperwork for a permit wasn't cleared up. The trouble was, she wasn't sure what Fredo was talking about and her father tended to do nothing but foam at the mouth and accuse Fredo of jealousy and double-dealing instead of taking care of the problem as he should.

It seemed to Isabella that control was slipping away. Without the special ingredient that set their sauce apart, there would be very little reason for anyone to choose their restaurant, Rosa, over the others operating nearby. She was desperate to get a handle on all these problems and get things back on an even keel.

Something had to be done.

She knew what it was. She had to go back there.

Just thinking about it made her shiver. She couldn't go back. The prince had explicitly ordered her to stay away. And for once in her life, she was not really ready to challenge that.

Odd as it seemed, he was so different, so separate from her way of life, that he threw her off balance in a way no other man had ever done. She was used to being the feisty

one, the girl who didn't accept any nonsense from men, the one who could take it, deal with it, and serve it right back A handsome face didn't bowl her over. Charm made her suspicious. The tough-guy act completely turned her off.

Isabella was a hard sell on every level. Life had made her that way. Though she looked happy and carefree to most who knew her casually, there was a thread of dread and unease in her soul that she'd come by naturally.

Her mother had died when she was three years old, leaving her the only female in the family. Her father and her two brothers immediately turned to her for everything. At the age of five she was already taking care of everyone else, in the family home, in the play yard, and even in the restaurant. People in the village called her "little Mama" as she scurried past on one errand or another. She was always in such a hurry to make things right for her little brothers, it seemed she never had time to have a childhood of her own.

But her unease and wistfulness were born of more than just too many responsibilities too early. There were uncertainties in her family background, half-remembered scenes from childhood, secrets and lies. Her mother's death, her father's sometimes mysterious background, the reason her baby brother Valentino carried his daredevil act too far, the reason her brother Cristiano felt he had to jump off cliffs to save lives—all these things and more created a shaky foundation for a calm, peaceful life.

Isabella had a recurring nightmare where her family restaurant began to sag, first on one side, then the other. Going outside, she would realize the building had been sitting on a sand dune and the sand was beginning to drain away. Frantically, she tried to shore it up with her hands, pushing the sand back, working faster and faster. But it was

no use. The building sank into the sand as though it were water. Inside she could see her father and her brothers trying to get out. She tried to call for help, but she couldn't make a sound. Helpless, she watched them disappear beneath the surface. And that was when she woke.

"You've obviously got a savior complex," Susa told her the one time she'd confided in the older woman. "Get over it. You can't save these people. We are each our own worst enemy."

Susa's words weren't very comforting. In fact, they weren't even very helpful. So she never told anyone about her dreams again. But she thought of them now as she tried to analyze what had happened last night.

As much as the dream unnerved her, misty memories of her night at the castle unsettled her even more. Had he really kissed her forehead or had she just wished so hard that she'd dreamed it? Had she really told him she'd thought he was a vampire for a few shattering seconds? Had she really reached out and stroked his scar as though she had a right to touch him? It didn't seem credible and it made her blush all over again.

She hadn't been herself last night. And that was one reason she hesitated to try to go back. What would he cause her to act like if she actually got in to see him again?

Meanwhile she had to deal with losing customers, losing money, and Fredo Cavelli coming by to threaten that he would have Rosa's closed down for good if her father didn't come up with some obscure piece of paper.

"He thinks he can order me around because he bribed the mayor to put him on the planning commission," Luca would scoff whenever she tried to talk to him about it. "I'm in compliance in every way. He can't run me out of town.

He's just jealous because the little ice cream store he tried to run fell apart in a month. I won't give in to his rubbish."

She shook her head and walked away, unsure of how threatening this business really was. She had more problems than she had time for, so she let it go. Meanwhile, several times a day, her gaze wandered toward the hills, searching out the mist-shrouded tower of the castle, just barely visible toward evening, and she wondered what Max was doing in his lonely sanctuary. Was he out riding again? Did he ever think of her? Or had he been so glad to be rid of her, he'd erased her from his mind?

Max was on horseback, surveying the river in the twilight magic that hovered over his land, just after sunset. His sister had gone home, his cousin was about to leave for Milan, and his life was about to get back to normal. Boring, monotonous normal. Still, it was a relief.

This was his favorite time of day, and the only time he found he could come to the river without feeling unbearably sick inside. And he had to come to the river, if only as an homage to Laura. For the first few years after her death, he hadn't been able to come here without tears flowing freely.

"I'm sorry," he would cry into the wind, brokenhearted and in agony. "I'm so sorry."

And he was convinced that Laura had been here then. She'd heard him. Later, he would often talk to her for hours, and she responded with a breeze, or a leaf that might sail over his head. He could hear her laughter in the river as the water bubbled over the rocks. She'd felt so close, he could almost touch her.

As the years went by the talking began to fade away, but he still came. And now, he didn't talk anymore. He didn't

feel her here as he had before. Maybe she'd lost interest. Maybe she'd forgotten him. Or maybe his emotions just weren't strong enough to break through the barriers any longer. He didn't know what it was that had silenced their conversation. He only knew it felt stilted and awkward to try to talk to her now. But he came anyway. She deserved that much, at the very least.

Tonight he was here in part out of a guilty conscience. His head had been full of the Casali girl for days and he couldn't seem to shake the thoughts away. He needed to fill his soul with his wife's image again.

He looked into the swirling water of the river, very near where that water had taken her from him.

"Laura," he said aloud, passion behind every word. "I miss you so."

He listened hard. He tried to let himself join the flow of the evening breeze. He tried to feel whatever was in the atmosphere and draw it in. But it was all a failure. She wasn't there. Heartsick, he turned his horse and headed back home.

Isabella had tried to figure out somehow to handle the declining basil supply problem in other ways, but the harder she tried, the more the answer seemed to elude her. As far as she knew, the prince's estate was the only site where the herb could be found. If she wasn't allowed to enter his gates, how was she going to get the supply she needed?

She spent hours poring over the Internet, trying to find where else the herb might grow, and, when that didn't yield fruit, trying to find a substitution. She tried a few candidates in a couple of dishes. People noticed.

"There's something different about this *Fruta di Mare*," an old friend of the family asked right away, frowning as

though she'd found a bug in her meal. "Have you changed your recipe?"

"What are you doing that's different?" another asked, face twisted with displeasure.

And then she overheard a pair of regular customers whispering to each other. The phrases she caught included, "This place used to be so good, it's really gone downhill lately," and she knew she was in big trouble.

There was no choice. She had to go back.

But how?

She was still agonizing over that a day later when a surprise visitor came through the doors of the café. The late afternoon sun made a radiating halo around him and for just a moment she was sure it was the prince himself. Her heart began to pound in her chest. She'd never felt such a lurch to her system before. The room tilted and for a beat or two she was sure she would pass out. But in those same seconds she realized it wasn't the prince at all, but his cousin, Marcello, and the pounding began to fade.

It took a minute for her to catch her breath. Even as she greeted him warmly she was clutching her heart and wondering what on earth was the matter with her. She really couldn't imagine. The prince was just a man. Nothing special. Particularly. She'd known men before and even liked a few of them. Not many, but a few. She quickly steadied herself and managed to smile at Marcello.

"Welcome. I'm so glad you decided to come try us. Please sit right here and let me bring you some wine."

She pulled out a chair at the table best situated with a view of the square in one direction and the distant mountains in the other.

"Order whatever you like," she said cheerfully. "It will be our pleasure to—"

"Whoa, slow down," he said with a laugh, raising both hands as though to defend himself from the onslaught. "I didn't come for free food. I'm on my way home to Milan, but I wanted to come by to see how my patient is doing."

"Patient?" And then she realized he meant her. "Oh, I'm fine. As you can see, I still have a black eye, but I've been told I look better this way, so it's not a problem."

He made a face at her lame joke, but went on. "And your stitches?"

"Oh."

"I'd like to take a look and see how they are healing."

She glanced around the restaurant. It wasn't packed by any means but half the tables were filled with people she'd known all her life. Every one of them was watching with rapt attention.

"Too public?" he asked as he followed her train of thought. She threw another quick look at the audience, then turned with a toss of her head.

"Let them talk," she said blithely. "TV is mostly reruns this week. They need some fresh entertainment."

He laughed and followed her to the storeroom where he looked her over and quickly pronounced her healing nicely. They chatted in the kitchen for a few minutes. She enjoyed being with him, but wasn't sure how to deal with that. He was so good-looking, but it was as if there was a special ingredient missing—just like the Rosa sauce without the *Monta Rosa Basil*. The prince had an element of fire in him that she found lacking in his cousin. There was no doubt about it—something about the Rossi prince appealed to her like no other man she'd ever seen.

"I want to ask you a question about your cousin," she told him at one point, a little hesitant. She knew it was going to be a touchy subject.

"Shoot," he said casually, cradling the glass of golden wine she'd poured for him.

"It's about his scars. I understand he was badly injured in a car accident. Is that true?"

Marcello nodded.

She frowned. "Why doesn't anyone seem to know anything about it here in the village?"

He shrugged. "People like the Rossi family have ways of keeping things quiet," he said. "And there were certain elements about that accident they didn't want the world to know about."

She drew her breath in. "Like what?" she asked.

He smiled. "Sorry, Isabella. That is not something I'm at liberty to talk about."

She leaned back, disappointed but intrigued. What could it possibly be?

But she had a more important question. How could she get his cousin to let her back on the royal property?

"If I could just talk to him," she said, searching Marcello's eyes for ideas. "If I could just explain how important this is."

He shrugged, draining the last drop of golden liquid from his glass. "Go on over and confront the lion in his lair," he suggested with a casual gesture appealing to the fates.

She scrunched up her face, a picture of doubt. "I don't think I'd better do that. I don't think that would really work. Besides, how would I get in?"

He shrugged again and straightened from his place at the counter. "Your call."

She sighed and gave him a significant look. "If only I had the number for his mobile."

"Ah." He bit back a grin, his eyes sparkling with laughter. "You're not the first to hint around for that number."

She leaned closer, trying to look persuasive but not sure how to do that with a man like this. "I'm sure you know what it is."

He nodded, looking her over with barely leashed pity. "I do. And I'm sworn to secrecy, just as you'd expect."

"Oh." She straightened and frowned, her heart sinking. "I'm not allowed to tell anyone."

She nodded, feeling tragic and hopeless. "I was afraid of that."

He looked as tragic as she felt. "I'm sorry. It would be a betrayal of trust for me to tell you what it is."

She nodded again, leaning against the tall counter with her chin in her hand. "I understand," she said sadly.

He reached past her to take a pencil from a cup full of them. "It's a fairly easy number to remember," he said as he pulled a piece of paper from a stack of them on the counter. "I think I could probably recreate it right now, just doodling here." And he began to do just that. "But I would never tell you what it is."

Her eyes widened. Had he just done what she thought he'd done? "Of course not," she said faintly, hope rekindled.

They chatted for another few seconds. Isabella was on tenterhooks but she studiously avoided looking at the paper in front of him, which he was filling with doodles. Still, she noticed out of the corner of her eye when he turned to leave and crushed it into a ball. Very deliberately, he tossed it into a nearby trash can.

"Take care, Isabella," he said. Giving her a big smile, he winked and headed for the door.

She waited until he was out of the room, then whirled and grabbed the paper from the trash can. She pressed it flat against the counter, and there it was—a telephone number, the figures embellished wildly, but still legible.

Just the thought of calling it sent her pulse soaring. Thanks to Marcello, she had what she'd wanted, a connection to the prince. Now, how was she going to work up the courage to use it?

Max jerked upright when he heard his mobile chime. For just a moment, he wondered what the noise was. He'd only heard it a few times before. Almost no one had his number, and those who did usually called on the landline or sent him an e-mail. He frowned as he fumbled through his stack of books and papers, looking for the blasted thing and ready to bark at whoever was calling and interrupting a good idea flow he'd got into on this lazy, sunny afternoon.

His frown deepened as he realized he didn't recognize the caller's ID. Probably a wrong number. He dropped the phone back onto his desk and turned away, ready to let it ring itself silly. But it didn't stop and he swore sharply and reached for it again, prepared to turn it off. But this time something about the caller ID caught his attention. He hesitated. Why not give it a try? After all, what could it hurt? With a grimace, he clicked on and put it to his ear.

"*Ciao.*"

There was a soft exhalation of breath and a feminine voice said, "Is this Max?"

He blinked. "Yes. Who's this?" But in a flash, he knew.

"Isabella Casali. I…we met the other night when I…"

Letting his head fall back, he closed his eyes. He really didn't need this. Life as he'd grown to know it was boring but placid. Not too many highs and lows—if you didn't count the midnight agonies of a guilty conscience. And then, this woman had inserted herself into his sphere. And it came to this—just the sound of her voice did strange and mystical things to him.

"I remember," he said gruffly. "How did you get this number?"

"It wasn't easy." She hesitated, then went on. "Listen, I don't mean to be a bother, but I need to talk to you."

His hand tightened on the small device. "It's that damned basil, isn't it?"

She sputtered for a few seconds, then got herself together again in time to be coherent. "Well, yes, it is. You see, this is a matter of such importance—"

He stopped her with a rude word. He was angry with himself, angry with her. The way she'd barged into his life a few nights before had affected him more than he wanted to admit. He told himself it was just her femaleness that had sent him into a tailspin for a couple of days.

It could have been any woman, anyone at all. Despite everything, he did feel a real lack of the feminine presence in his life. He missed having someone around who put flowers in a glass and plunked them in the middle of the table at breakfast. He missed the flow of shiny hair spilling over a smooth, silky shoulder, the soft pout of red, swollen lips, the cheerful voice that sounded like sunshine, the way a pair of breasts filled out a sweater and pulled the fabric in that tightly entrancing way that just knocked him out. All these things shouted femininity to him. Having a woman around made daily existence softer, more colorful, more dramatic. He missed that.

But such things were part of a life that was closed to him now. Finding Isabella on his property had just brought that home to him and made the loss fresh again. He needed to forget all about her.

And he'd managed over the last few days to practically obliterate her from his consciousness. He'd done it deliberately, piece by piece, setting up work schedules and

exercise routines that demanded more of his attention and time, until he fell exhausted into bed at night and slept like a drugged beast. He'd done everything he could think of to make his life new and challenging in order to keep his mind from going where he didn't need it to go.

Now here she was with her provocative voice and her urgent requests, stirring up things he didn't want stirred. That made him angry, even though a part of him knew that the anger was a direct attempt to stave off temptation.

"Tell me the truth," he demanded. "How did you get this number?"

She drew her breath in. "I found it."

The sheer audacity of that answer took him by surprise and he nearly laughed out loud. But he held it back and managed to ask with a straight face, "Where?"

"In the trash."

He shook his head. Did she really think he was going to buy that one? "Isabella, please. That doesn't make any sense."

She sighed. "Life doesn't make any sense. Hadn't you noticed?"

"Don't try to throw sand in my eyes with ridiculous philosophical musings," he warned her, thoroughly annoyed. "This is a very basic problem. It doesn't need an esoteric response. You found my number. I want to know how so that it doesn't happen again."

"I've told you the truth," she insisted, sounding earnest. "It was in my trash."

So she wasn't going to tell him. That only strengthened his convictions. If she couldn't respond truthfully to a simple question, he didn't need her complicating his life any longer. Best to cut all ties as quickly as possible. Prolonging this would only make things worse for him and his peace of mind.

"I don't know how you got this number," he told her gruffly, "but it hardly matters. I'll get it changed right away."

She drew her breath in. "All so you can avoid any calls from me?" she asked, her voice sounding shocked.

"Yes," he said stoutly.

She didn't understand. But that was for the best. If she ever tumbled to the truth—that she affected him as no one else had in years—his situation would be that much more precarious.

"Why do you hate me?" she asked, aghast.

"I don't hate you." He groaned softly, closing his eyes. "That's just the problem," he muttered under his breath.

"What?" she said.

He gritted his teeth and expelled a long line of swear words in an obscure dialect, just because it made him feel better. This woman was driving him around the bend. And that was odd. He didn't remember trouble like this with women that he'd known before…before Laura. He'd always had friends and casual relationships. It seemed he'd lost the knack for free and easy dealings with the opposite sex.

Of course, Laura's death and the accident that had scarred him had changed all that. For over a year after it had happened, he hadn't been able to speak to anyone, even family members. He had waited to die, wishing for it. When that didn't happen, he began to realize he was going to have to go on without her and without his face. And that was a problem. He didn't have much appetite for it.

It had taken a long time, but slowly he had let others in—but only his immediate family and a few close friends. Most other friends had probably decided he must be dead himself. He didn't really want them around and that had become obvious.

And no strangers. Never strangers.

Yet, once he'd opened up to his closest family members, he'd begun to see that there were still things he could do with his life, even if he didn't go out into the world as before. Today, he had a relatively active professional life, thanks to the computer and the Internet. In the old days, he would probably have been locked away from all human commerce, but with the modern conveniences of semi-anonymous communication he was able to do quite a bit without having to come face-to-face with the people he interacted with. Mostly, he still only saw people he'd known all his life.

"That's because you're a coward," his sister maintained wryly during one of their frequent arguments.

He didn't take offense. She was probably right. Though he told himself he didn't want to inflict his savaged visage on others, that was only a part of it. He didn't want to see the reaction in the eyes of strangers. There was a certain vanity there, he had to admit. But he knew what the world wanted from him, and it wasn't his scarred face.

He'd been through the fickle reactions of the public at large before and he knew very well how cruel they could be. His mother had been a beautiful film star. During her twenties and early thirties, people had flocked to see her films. She'd been in demand everywhere.

But unlucky genetics had been her downfall. She had lost her looks early. Even as a young boy he'd understood how the media had begun to rip apart her image as she had disappointed them. It almost seemed they took it personally that she wasn't the beauty she once had been. As though she'd wasted their time and now would have to pay the price. He had been ten years old when she had taken her own life.

Yes, he knew what the public was like. And he didn't see any reason why he should go out of his way to be accepted by them again.

But Isabella Casali was another matter. He couldn't seem to put her off in a distant box the way he knew he ought to.

He came back to the conversation, knowing he needed to create a plausible alternative to her accusation of him hating her. "I hate talking on the phone," he supplied quickly. "It's not just you," he added.

Despite everything, he didn't want to hurt her. She was quite adorable and didn't deserve it. This was *his* problem, not hers. If only he could explain to her… But that was impossible. "I don't like talking to anyone."

"Oh."

She still sounded downhearted and that made him wince. Silently, he told himself to man up. He had to remain firm. It was the only way.

"Well, I won't keep you much longer," she promised, sounding wistful. "I just have one thing to talk to you about."

He knew what that was. There was no point prolonging things. "The answer is no," he said evenly.

"But you don't know—"

"Yes, I do. You want permission to come in and scavenge my river valley hillside for your precious basil herb. And I won't allow it. Case closed."

He could almost hear her gulp and he grimaced. He hated doing this. He could see the look she probably had in her huge blue eyes and it killed him. But he couldn't weaken.

"Please hear me out—"

"No, I won't allow it. It's too dangerous."

It was her turn to make that sound of exasperation. "Dangerous? What's dangerous about it?"

"You fell into the river, didn't you?"

"Yes, but that was because it was the middle of the night and you scared me."

He nodded. "Exactly. These things are always…accidents." He should just hang up and he knew it. He tried. But somehow, it just seemed too cruel.

"Why?" Her voice sharpened, as though she'd suddenly found the hint of a chink in his argument. "Why are you so sure I'll get hurt? Has anyone actually been hurt in that river?"

His throat choked shut for a moment. This was something he couldn't talk about. He closed his eyes for a moment and took a deep breath to steady his resolve. The consequences were too risky to gamble with.

There was a part of him, in a deep, secret place, that halfway believed there was an evil force lurking by the river, waiting to trap another woman—especially one that he had some affection for—and pull her under the water as well. There was another, more rational part of him that contended the evil force was his own sense of guilt. Which side was right? It wasn't worth putting it to the test.

"Isabella, I forbid you to go anywhere near that hillside. And the river. Stay away."

"But—"

"Promise me." His voice was harsh and stern. He had to make sure she didn't feel she could come on her own.

She swallowed hard. He could hear the effort she was making but that didn't matter. He steeled himself. It had to be done.

"All right," she said at last in a very small voice. "I'll stay away. At least I'll stay away until I can find a way to convince you—"

"You're not going to convince me. I'm changing this number, remember?"

"But, Max…"

He winced. Hearing his name in her voice sent a quiver through him, a sense of something edgy that he didn't like at all. Given a little time, it would chip away at his resolve, bit by bit.

"Goodbye, Isabella," he said firmly.

She sighed. "Goodbye."

Her voice had a plaintive quaver that touched his heart, but he hung up anyway. He had to. Another moment or two and he'd have been giving in to her, and that was something that couldn't happen.

This entire connection had to end. He couldn't afford the time and emotional effort involved in maintaining a relationship, even on the phone. He had work to do.

But returning to his research was hopeless at this point. Instead, he rose, grabbed his towel and headed for the fully equipped gym he'd had built into half of the whole ground level of the building. It was obvious he was going to have to fight harder to push Isabella Casali out of his system.

CHAPTER FIVE

ISABELLA fought back tears of frustration as she clicked off her phone connection to the palazzo.

"There go any hopes of a career in negotiations," she muttered to herself. "Turns out I'm not any better at that than I am at breaking and entering."

Hardly a surprise, but disappointing anyway. What now? Giving up wasn't an option. One look at her half-empty restaurant told her that. She was going to have to find another way. But how? She'd promised him she wouldn't go near the hillside or the river and she was going to keep that promise, much as it hurt.

But there had to be a way to breach those high walls in a more effective manner. Someone in the village had to have dealings with the palazzo. It didn't make sense that they would import everything from Rome. Slowly, carefully, she began to ask around. At first all she got were blank stares.

And then, finally, she hit pay dirt of a sort. Much to her surprise, the man who delivered seafood to her restaurant every morning also made a stop at the Rossi palazzo once or twice a week.

"Only on Tuesdays and Fridays," he told her chattily,

wiping his hands on his big white apron. "Wednesdays are out. It seems to be the day off for the staff, such as it is."

"Really?"

"Oh, yes. I made the mistake of showing up on a Wednesday once. I couldn't even get in the gate. I had two pounds of Chilean sea bass go bad over that little error."

"Do you ever see the prince?" she asked quickly, afraid he might escape before she got all she needed to know from him.

"The prince?" He shrugged. "I don't think so. I usually deal with an old fellow who tries to get something for nothing every time." He chuckled. "The place is like a mausoleum. You'd think it was full of old dead ancestors, but somebody seems to have an appetite for salmon and scallops."

And so, a plan was born.

The gap in the stone wall that surrounded the Rossi estate was still there. No one had filled it in—and that was lucky. Without this little piece of access, her plan would never have worked at all.

And so the following Wednesday, Isabella squeezed through and then stood very still in the warm noon sun, listening as hard as she could. The wind was quiet. The water was a distant babbling. And once the pounding of her heart quieted down, she could tell—the guard dogs didn't seem to be loose. There wasn't a sign of them.

She bit her lip, tempted to race up the hill and gather basil as fast as she could, then race back again. But she knew that was no solution. And such an action certainly held no honor. Much as the prince scared her, she had to confront him about this and do things openly and honestly.

He'd told her not to come here. She had to change his mind—not steal from him. Taking a deep breath, she started up the hill toward the castle.

It was a long climb and she was carrying a heavy back-pack with supplies—her special sauce pan, her favorite olive oil, the tomatoes that would form her base—and a small container of all that was left of the basil supply for her restaurant. She was going to go for broke and cook for the prince. It was pretty much the last idea she had left.

All the way, she kept expecting to hear someone shouting for her to go back. That didn't happen and she found some shade once she'd reached the top of the hill. There were no cars in sight, and not a sign of life anywhere. The castle looked just as old and moldy, but a lot less intimidating in the sunlight.

A few minutes of rest and she began to work up the nerve to go on with her plan. She knew where the cook's entrance was. She would use that first, hoping to find things unlocked. Once she was inside, she knew exactly what to do next.

She scanned the windows as high as she could look. There was no telling where his rooms were, no way to know where he hung out during the day.

Her fingers trembled a bit as she reached for the latch on the kitchen door, and she paused for a moment. Closing her eyes, she muttered a quick plea. This had to work. He had to understand. He was a prince, but he was also a man and she was counting on that basic humanity to come through for her in the end.

And whatever chance there was, she had to take it. She had no choice.

Max stood with his eyes closed and savored being bombarded by water. He'd just had a grueling workout in his gym and the water pouring over his naked body was creating a special kind of ecstasy. Every aching muscle

sang with relief. Every body part relaxed with delight. Every nerve, every fiber, came together in rapt happiness.

He would have to pay for this someday. Maybe at the gates of heaven. This was pure self-indulgence and he was probably wasting water to boot, but he let it go on and on, gushing through his thick hair, making small silver rivers over his tanned shoulders and through the dark thatch on his chest. It felt so damn good. He was pure appetite today, appetite for pleasure.

And what the hell? It was his birthday.

It was his birthday and no one had remembered.

That was okay. In fact, it was exactly as he wanted it to be. He hated people making a fuss. What was a birthday, anyway? Just a day. Nothing special. All the celebrating was just a pretence that something had actually happened, something had actually changed, a milestone had been set down. And actually, it was all much ado about nothing.

A memory floated into his mind, how his birthday had been when Laura was still with him. She'd slipped out of bed early in the morning and taken little gifts and hidden them all over the castle. It had taken him the entire day to find them all. How she'd laughed when he'd looked in all the wrong places. He could almost hear her musical voice now.

But he shook it away. Thinking of Laura was still too painful. Would there ever come a time when he could remember her without that dull, hopeless, agonizing pain of guilt in his gut?

Finally he was ready to put a stop to this and get on with his day. He turned off the water and stood there for a moment, feeling the mist around him turn into clear air, the warmth turn into refreshing coolness, the moisture evaporate on his skin. For some reason his senses seemed especially acute today. He was feeling things he never noticed,

hearing birds outside, feeling a breeze, enjoying the rays of the sun that came in through the open window. As usual, he avoided looking in the mirror while he dried himself with a huge fluffy towel, glancing out the window at the beautiful day instead.

"There's no place like Italy," he murmured to himself. "And in Italy, there's no place like Monta Correnti."

He stretched in the warm sunlight, smelling the clean scent of his soap. And…something else.

He stopped, frowning, and sniffed the air again. There was something else in the wind—or, more likely, wafting up from the kitchen. Someone was cooking. How could someone be cooking? There was no one here. Even Renzo was gone, making his weekly trip to see his daughter an hour's drive away.

Was it his imagination?

No, it got stronger. Garlic, tomatoes, olive oil, and something else.

It was a wonderful smell. A slow smile began to transform his face. It seemed someone had remembered his birthday after all and had come back to surprise him. It had to be Renzo.

Much as the old sourpuss tended to be a dour figure, he had his moments. Max pulled on a pair of jeans, suddenly in a hurry to find out what was going on. He turned to the stairway, bounding down, barefooted and shirtless, feeling happier than he'd felt in a long time. Funny how the fact that someone had remembered his birthday after all seemed to buoy him. He was smiling as he pushed in through the swinging doors to the kitchen.

"So you did remember my birthday after all," he said, and then he stopped dead, shocked to the core. It wasn't Renzo who turned to greet him.

"You!" He stared at her. "How did you get in here?"

Isabella was opening her mouth, and as she did so she thought she had words to say. But somehow they never made it out past her lips. For the moment, she couldn't speak.

It was all too much. She was startled by the way he'd come barging into the room, but, more than that, she was stunned at the beauty of the man she saw before her. His bare chest, his strong shoulders and muscular arms, the way his worn jeans rode low on his hips, revealing a tanned stomach that was smooth and tight as a trampoline canvas, all combined to present a picture of raw, candid masculinity that took her breath away.

"Oh! I…I…"

His jaw was hard as stone and his eyes blazed. "What the hell are you doing here?"

"Uh…" She gestured toward the stove. "Cooking?"

His head went back. That part was obvious. He was tensed, every muscle hardening, as though ready to pick her up physically and throw her out onto the front walkway.

"That's not what I mean," he said through teeth that were close to clenched.

"I know. I know."

She shook her head, trying to clear it. She'd never responded to a man like this before. She was swooning like a young girl in the sixties at a Beatles concert. She had to get a grip.

But something about him had hit her hard, right in the emotions. He had come barging into the kitchen and as she'd turned to greet him she'd seen this beautifully sculptured image of a man, backlit by the golden light coming in from the high windows. Michelangelo's creation in the flesh. She had that feeling she sometimes got when her favorite tenor reached an impossibly high note and held it

forever. She even had tears stinging in her eyes—he was just so beautiful.

She turned from him and leaned against the counter, her hand over her mouth. Staring into the red sauce bubbling on the stove, she fought for stability. What was she going to do? She couldn't seem to stay sane around this man.

And she had to. This was not what she'd come for. She didn't want to be mesmerized by his male appeal. She had a case to make and she had to stay on her toes to make it. But somehow sanity and the prince didn't seem to go together well.

Too bad, she told herself sternly. *You've got to do this right.*

Taking a deep breath, she turned back to face him. Resolutely, she lifted her gaze and stared at him hard.

"Okay, here's the deal," she said, and somehow she managed to sound strong. "You are denying me access to something I need in order to survive. Something my family traditionally has had access to. We have to find a way to compromise on this."

He stared back at her. She was looking up at him, her eyes very wide, and he realized he hadn't even thought to shield his face from her gaze. Here he was in broad daylight with none of the protective shadows of the other night. And there she was, staring straight at him. And yet, once again he felt no overwhelming need to turn away as he felt so often with others. Her gaze was open and natural. She might be scared of something about him, but it wasn't his face.

But it was *her* face that drew his attention. He took a step closer and reached out to take her chin in his hand and tilt her head so that he could examine her. And then he swore softly.

"Isabella, you still have a bad bruise," he said, a touch of outrage in his voice as he studied her black eye.

"Oh," she said, blinking rapidly. "Yes, I've been told it will take a while to fade."

He swore softly, shaking his head, then pulled away from her and looked at the items she'd spread out all over the kitchen.

"You're going to have to pack all this up and get out of here," he said tersely.

She took a step back away from him. She knew he was angry at finding her here. What confused her a bit, though, was why her black eye seemed to make him even angrier. As though it were her fault or something!

"Why?"

He looked back at her. "Because, once again, you're trespassing. You're going to have to go."

She shook her head. She wasn't going to be bowled over so easily. She lifted her chin. "Not until you try the sauce."

A look of surprise flashed in his dark eyes. He turned to glance at the brew simmering in the pot. "Is this your special sauce?"

"Yes."

He turned back and met her defiant eyes.

"I don't want to try your sauce, Isabella. I'm sure it's a fine sauce. But, no matter how good it is, it won't change anything. The special quality of your sauce is not at issue here. It's the access to the hillside, and I can't allow you to go there."

He was like a stone wall. Her hope began to flag.

"Max, please." She winced and drew back a bit. "Don't you understand?" she said, trying hard to be calm and reasonable. "I have to go there."

He shrugged as though he just didn't care. "I'm going to go and finish dressing," he said dryly. "I expect you to have cleared out by the time I get back."

He began to turn away.

Isabella cried out. "No!"

He hesitated and looked back, and in that same moment a furious Isabella, all tossed hair and flashing eyes, got between him and the doorway before he realized what was happening.

"You listen to me," she demanded, jabbing a finger against his naked chest. "It wasn't easy doing this. It wasn't easy coming all this way and climbing the hill with all these supplies, or finding the right time to come here when I would be able to get in, and preparing myself and putting together a proper case to make to convince you. You can at least pay me the respect of hearing me out."

He grabbed her hand to stop the jabbing and ended up holding onto it. "Why should I hear you out? Your problems have nothing to do with me."

"Yes, they do," she insisted, trying to free her hand from his grip. "You own the hillside where the basil grows. That herb is the linchpin of my family's existence. Without it, our restaurant is over and my father's lifework is in ruins."

She finally yanked her hand away and jabbed him again. "You will listen," she demanded, her eyes fierce.

Max hadn't been around many people for a good long time, but he'd always had a knack for understanding a lot about human psychology. One thing he knew was that, faced with someone who was almost overwrought with passionate intensity, the worst thing you could do was to laugh. It drove the person crazy and it made you look like a jerk. He knew it was all wrong. Not to mention, if your goal was to calm the person down, it just plain didn't work very well.

But he couldn't help it. She looked so cute. Her curly hair was flopping down over her huge eyes and her cheeks

were bright red and her lips looked lusciously swollen. And she was so earnest.

He started to try to answer her, but the words didn't come out right. What did come out was a choking laugh, and once it got started he had a hard time getting it stopped again.

Laughing. It was something he never did. As he tried to analyze it later, he decided it was a release of sorts. He'd spent so long being so tense, so filled with anguished guilt, and Isabella had reached into his life and pulled aside the curtain, letting in a ray of sunshine that helped open the floodgates to emotions he had kept bottled up for too long. But once those gates had opened, it was hard getting them closed again.

She stood back, stunned, her blue eyes bewildered. Next she was going to look hurt and he knew it. He didn't want her to be hurt. He had to stop that. He had to tell her, had to explain…

But he was laughing and, for the moment, all he could do was reach for her and fold her into his arms.

"How dare you?" she cried, struggling against him.

"Hush, hush," he was saying, stroking her hair and leaning down into the crook of her neck to drop a kiss on her tender skin, his lips lingering a moment or two too long. His whole purpose was to calm her down, of course, and to reassure her that he wasn't laughing at her. Not really. But her neck was so inviting and her skin tasted so sweet and he found himself dropping more kisses than he'd ever meant to, dropping them lightly at first, then with more and more intensity, letting his tongue flicker on her skin.

"I'm sorry, Isabella," he murmured against her warmth, still racked with humor. "I don't mean to laugh. It's not that I'm laughing *at* you. Honestly, I'm really not…"

"I hate you!" she cried, still trying to break free. "You're mean and arrogant and—"

"No," he said, finally getting control of the laughter and pulling up to look at her. "No, listen…"

She shook her head and her hair flew around her face. There were tears in her eyes. His heart melted at the sight.

"Oh, Isabella," he said gruffly, full of regret. "No, I didn't mean to laugh."

Her lower lip was trembling. He cupped her face in his hands. She was beautiful and he moved purely by instinct. She had a spirit that had to be soothed, a mouth that had to be kissed. There was no stopping it. Nature had taken over.

CHAPTER SIX

UNPLANNED passion like this was taboo, unacceptable—
and, once ignited, completely irresistible. Max's lips
touched Isabella's once, twice, and then again, as though
he'd suddenly developed a raving hunger for the taste of
her, and then the moist warmth of her mouth was there,
open and inviting and his kiss grew in sweet, silky intensity. And he was lost in the moment.

It was hard to know how long the kiss lasted. When he
finally revived, feeling like a swimmer coming up for air,
she was trying to push him away and murmuring, "No, no.
I didn't come here for this."

He pulled his face back, but his fingers were still tangled
in her hair. He looked down at her and shook his head
almost sadly.

"Neither did I," he told her, his gaze ranging over her
pretty face. It took all his strength to keep from kissing
her again. "But I won't say I'm sorry it happened," he
added, his voice husky with the lingering sense of how
tempting she was.

Their eyes met. He saw wonder there, and questions.
She was a woman who deserved more than he was allowing
her. He groaned, then shrugged in bittersweet surrender.

"All right, Isabella. I'm ready to sample your sauce and hear your entire presentation."

Suddenly her face was shining. "That's all I ask," she said, blooming like a flower that had just found the sun. "Just give me half an hour."

He nodded, reluctantly smiling at the picture she made. "You've got it. Hit me with your best shot." He gave her a warning look. "And then I will tell you 'no' and send you home again."

She nodded happily. "I'll convince you. You just wait."

He released her slowly, wishing he could pull her back into his arms and hold her again. Somehow he doubted her cooking was going to captivate him more strongly than her kisses had.

He went back to his room to put on a shirt and she got busy cooking the pasta. She'd actually talked him into hearing her out. She could hardly believe it.

The fact that he'd kissed her didn't mean a thing, she told herself. It had thrilled her and she was still tingling. Her heart was racing, skittering around like a happy bird in her chest. But she knew she shouldn't have let it happen and now she had to get over it. She had work to do.

But she also knew that she would be remembering how her cheek had felt against his naked chest for the rest of her life. The smoothness of his skin, the strength of his arms, the sound of his heartbeat, had sent her into a tailspin. She had to push those thoughts away, save them for later, or she wouldn't be able to do what she'd set out to.

He was more beautiful, more manly, more exciting than any man she'd ever known, but, still, she hadn't let it completely drag her under, and she was proud of that. She'd been the one to pull away. And she had definitely not come

here scheming to use any feminine wiles or anything of the sort. The kiss hadn't been planned by either of them and it didn't count.

At least, she hoped it didn't. Because she wasn't going to let it happen again. She couldn't.

Taking a deep breath, she nodded. Never again. That was the route to ruin and she was too smart to go that way. She had something to accomplish here, and she got down to it.

Max sat at the head of the long mahogany table that had been in his family for over two hundred years. Before him lay a mat of ivory lace that was set with heavy sterling silver flatware in an exceptionally beautiful baroque pattern. Two crystal goblets of wine had been added, one reflecting a golden hue, the other taking in sunlight and translating it into a deep, rich, royal red. There was a silver fingerbowl as well, deeply engraved with a bucolic scene, and a fine, creamy-white, linen napkin.

He surveyed it all and shook his head, wondering how she'd found everything so quickly. It had been almost thirty years since he'd seen these pieces laid out this way—when his mother was alive.

It came to him that he ought to do this more often. Just seeing these things here, touching them, brought up feelings of attachment, memories of ancestors, connections to his family and his past that he didn't think about often enough. It all touched a chord deep inside him, a link to eternity.

He swallowed his smile quickly as Isabella entered the room. Sunlight slanted in from the tall windows that lined the space, setting her dark hair aflame with golden highlights. Her cheeks were red from time over a hot stove and she was carrying a steaming pot with hot pads protecting

her hands. As she approached, the scent of something extraordinary filled the room.

He shook his head. As he watched her a sense of her beauty overwhelmed him, despite her bruised eye, and he felt an intense need to hold her again that filled him with an aching regret.

How had he gotten here? It was insane. Over the last few years, he'd lived his whole life to keep people away. Isabella had somehow crept right through his barriers and found the center of his being in ways no one else had done. He wasn't really sure how she'd accomplished that, but he knew she had. And he knew he had to resist it.

She turned an impish smile his way as she placed the pot onto the trivet in the middle of the table.

"There you are," she told him, ladling the sublime sauce out into a porcelain bowl, which she'd already filled with freshly made pasta. "I hope you'll deem this fit for a king," she said with another grin. "Or, at any rate, a prince."

He looked down into the bowl. The sauce was the color of a late summer sunset and swimming with beautiful vegetables he couldn't name. "It smells wonderful."

She nodded and didn't waste time on false modesty. "It tastes wonderful, too."

He managed to maintain a skeptical look, just for dignity's sake. "We'll see."

And he began to eat.

She was right. The sauce filled his mouth with a feeling like ecstasy. He'd never had anything quite like it. Amazing how one little herb could make such a difference.

"Well?" she asked, watching him like a hawk.

He looked at her. He could hardly keep his eyes off her. She was so alive, so vibrant, so expressive. There was something real about her, something basic and decent and

appealing in a new way. He felt a pull toward her, a definite attraction, something he couldn't deny.

But how could that be? She was so different from the wife he had loved so much. The woman he still missed so much.

Laura had been blonde, ethereal, slender and light as a bird. She had looked very much in life like the angel she had surely become since. But this woman was very different—full and round and earthy. And, to his eternal regret, he ached for her right now as he'd seldom ached for a woman before.

He looked back down at the bowl, avoiding her bright gaze. It was insane to let her stay. He had to get her out of here before he lost control and did something crazy.

The worst of it was, it was quite evident that she had not come here to seduce him at all. She was dressed modestly in a simple peasant blouse and full skirt. There was no cleavage showing, no revealing exposure of skin. She was honest and straightforward and she wasn't playing games. He liked her for that. It showed a certain respect for him and for the dilemma between them. The fact that he could detect the beauty of her body beneath all the swishing fabric was beside the point. She wasn't using it as a trump card— even though she probably sensed it wouldn't be hard to do.

Resolutely he lifted his gaze and met hers.

"*Magnifico*, Isabella," he told her. "This is spectacular. I can fully understand why your cuisine is famous and people come from miles around to enjoy it."

She brightened with happiness at his words. "You've heard of it, then?"

"Oh, yes," he admitted.

She radiated joy. "I knew once you tried it—"

"And I understand how important it is to you," he interrupted before she could have a chance to make assumptions

his admission didn't quite warrant. "But that doesn't change the danger that you would face every time you went across that divide above the river." His hand swept out in a royal gesture. "If I had a house full of servants, I could have one of them go and harvest the weed for you. But at present, Renzo and I live here alone. There is no one to help out."

Isabella bit down hard on her lower lip, keeping herself under tight control. His constant emphasis on the danger of going near the river was clearly overstated and there had to be a reason for it. She was pretty sure it had something to do with the death of his wife. What had happened that had made him so sure the place wasn't safe for her? She wanted to know, but she didn't want to push him. A horrible vision of tractors mowing down the hillside if he got annoyed enough did the trick.

Back to the plan.

"We can talk about that later," she said quickly. "Right now I just want you to enjoy this."

He gave her a faint, reluctant smile, his eyes glowing. "I do, Isabella. More than you know."

She flushed. It was odd to watch how he still tended to turn his face away from her, as though trying to keep her from seeing the scars. No matter what he did, he looked gorgeous to her. How could it be otherwise when he was blessed with those huge, emotional dark eyes and that wide, sensual mouth?

He looked like a poet, she decided. A poet with a tender, sensitive soul purposefully disguised by his muscular form and his harsh, cynical manner, all protected by a wall of ice to keep the world at bay. She knew about his physical scars. What had hurt him so deeply that he couldn't be free? That was the mystery he carried with him.

"Tell me about this place," she said, leaning forward on her elbows as she watched him eat. "Did you grow up here?"

"Pretty much." He took another bite, savored it, and sighed with pleasure, then went on. "My father tended to drag us all over the continent, staying at one property after another. He was quite a gambler, you see, and he was always looking for another game. But when I was young we spent a lot of time here. I would ride my pony all over these grounds."

"Mmm. And you didn't fall into the river?"

His face darkened. "That is not a matter to joke about," he said curtly. "Our river is a dangerous place. We didn't realize how dangerous at the time." He looked at her face and winced. "I should have caught you before you hit the rocks."

She marveled at him. He seemed to think it was his job to save the world—or at least all females that came within his purview. That was too big a role to take on for any man. She wished she knew how to tell him so. Instead, she shrugged.

"It will heal. It will be gone in no time at all."

He heard her blithe words but they didn't placate him. He couldn't help but feel that the water had almost claimed another victim that night. If he hadn't been there to grab her…

He shook his head again and swore softly.

"And as you grew older?" she asked. "Did you still stay here often?"

He pushed away thoughts of the river and let himself look back instead. "Not as often. My mother died when I was young and, after that, I went to live with my aunt, Marcello's mother."

"I'm sorry," she murmured about his mother. She hesitated to tell him they had something in common. Was she being presumptuous? Never mind, she told him anyway.

"I lost my mother early, too," she told him. "I can hardly remember what she looked like."

"Where were you sent to live?" he asked.

She shrugged. "I stayed right where I was. Someone had to take care of my father, and my two little brothers."

He stared. "Surely you were a little young for that."

She smiled. "Yes, much too young. But we didn't have a choice. We didn't have the money or the other 'properties' like you did. We made do."

His face twisted. "You mean, *you* made do. But at least you had your family around you."

She looked up, surprised. "Where was your father?"

He gazed at her coolly. "He was despondent. My mother's death hit him hard." His gaze darkened. "We didn't see much of him after that."

"But you had your sister."

He shook his head. "Not really. She went to live with another aunt. I had a pretty lonely childhood when you come right down to it. You were lucky to stay with your family, even if it did mean you ended up being the support for everyone." He smiled at her. "That was the way it was, wasn't it?"

She frowned, feeling bad for him. At least she had her father and had benefited from his love and counsel all her life. She didn't know how she would have made it without that. Hearing about his experiences gave her a new perspective on what family could mean to a child.

"But I soon went away to school in Switzerland," he continued, "and then to university in England. And then… then I married."

The young wife he'd lost tragically. Should she say anything? She wasn't sure, so she murmured condolences again, and he brushed them aside.

"Never mind all that," he said crisply, looking at her over the rim of his wine glass. "Tell me more about you, Isabella. Tell me about your hopes and dreams and how many young men you've been in love with."

Here was the opening she'd been waiting for.

"Exactly what I planned to do," she told him cheerfully. "Well, not counting the boyfriends. They shall remain nameless, if you don't mind." She made a face at him. "But while you're finishing your meal, I'm going to give you a small background about my family and our restaurant." She gave a little bow. "With your permission," she added pertly.

He waved a hand her way, his attention back on the delicious food before him.

"Carry on," he said kindly.

"Thank you." She settled into the chair that faced his. "First about my father. His name is Luca Casali. His mother, Rosa, started a restaurant here in Monta Correnti after her husband died and left her with a young family to support. She used a special recipe she got from a secret source, and her food was well received."

He looked up with a slight smile, his gaze skimming over her face. He liked the way she talked. She was so animated.

"So you are from a restaurant family from the beginning, aren't you?"

She scrunched up her face a bit. "More or less. My father and his sister, Lisa, took over my grandmother's restaurant when she died, but they don't get along very well, so they split up. My father had a roadside stand for years before he moved to our current location. My aunt still runs Sorella, which is basically my grandmother's place updated for modern times."

She pulled a scrapbook out of her bag and put it on the

table, close to his mat. She'd put it together, using the computer to blow up pictures that would illustrate her family history and help Max understand what Rosa, and the special herb, meant to them all.

"Here is a picture of my father as a young man when he had the food stand on the Via Roma. And the next picture was taken when he was finally able to open a real restaurant, the place we call Rosa, after my grandmother, the culmination of all his hard work."

Max turned and leaned forward, taking the book from her and frowning at the first picture she'd turned to.

"This is your father?" he asked.

"Yes. Luca Casali."

He nodded slowly. "I remember him. He used to come here when I was a child."

Isabella stared at him. This was the first she'd heard of such a thing. "Here? To the Rossi palazzo?"

"Yes." He looked at her, noting an element or two of resemblance to the man. "I think he cooked for us occasionally."

She suddenly felt a bit smaller than before, reminded that she was from a different world than the one this man was from.

"Oh," she said, looking around the cavernous room and trying unsuccessfully to picture her father here. But she took a deep breath and went back to her story.

"Here is a picture of my aunt Lisa. Do you know her, too?"

He looked at the picture and shook his head. "No. I don't think I've ever seen her before."

For some reason, that was a huge relief to her.

"Good," she muttered, turning pages. "Here are my brothers, Cristiano and Valentino."

Max nodded, his interest only barely retained. "Nice-

looking young men," he murmured, looking back at what was left of his pasta.

"*Very* nice-looking young men," she corrected. She was crazy about her brothers. "They are both away. Cristiano is a firefighter. He's in Australia right now, helping them with their terrible brush fires. And Valentino is a race-car driver. He's always somewhere racing around trying to challenge death at every turn."

He raised his head in surprise at the bitterness of her tone, and she smiled quickly to take the edge off it.

"So neither one is here helping run the restaurant," he noted.

"That's what my father has me for," she maintained stoutly. "But I do wish they would come home more often."

"Of course."

"And finally, here is a picture of Rosa as it was two months ago, when we still had a plentiful stock of the basil. See how crowded it is? Doesn't everyone look well fed and happy?"

He laughed softly at her characterization. "Yes," he admitted. "I see what you mean."

"And here is the restaurant now." She plunked down a picture of the half-empty room and threw out her hands to emphasize how overwhelming the situation was. "Without the basil, no one is happy anymore."

He groaned, turning his head and refusing to study that last picture. "Isabella, I get the point. You don't have to rub my nose in it."

"It seems I do." She gazed at him fiercely. "I want you to understand how important this is. How it means everything to my father."

"And to you."

"To me?" She pressed her lips together and thought

about it. Hearing his words surprised her, but what surprised her even more was that he might be right.

For years she'd chafed at being the one everybody depended on, the one who had to stay behind and help with the restaurant while her brothers went off in search of adventurous lives and her cousins went off to explore places like England and Australia. Isabella was the one who stayed home and kept the flames going. Sometimes it didn't seem fair. She'd had daydreams about leaving a note pinned to her pillow and slipping out into the night, getting on a train to Rome, flying to Singapore or Brazil, or maybe even New York. Meeting a dark, handsome stranger in an elevator. Talking over a drink in a hotel bar. Walking city streets in the rain, sharing an umbrella. All scenes snatched from romantic movies, all scenes folded into her momentary fantasies. What seemed hopeful at first eventually mutated into melancholy as it aged.

And lately, even those dreams had faded. She'd been as wrapped up in finding ways to save the restaurant as her father was. So maybe Max was right. Maybe it did mean everything to her, too.

"Maybe," she said faintly.

What did it mean when you gave up your dreams? Did they grow mellow and rich, like fine wine, warming you even as they faded? Or did they dry up and turn to powder that blew away with the wind?

"Maybe."

Snapping back into the moment, she looked at Max, trying to see if he'd come around yet. She grimaced lightly. It certainly didn't look like it. Those gorgeous dark eyes with their long, sweeping lashes were as cool and skeptical as ever.

She sighed. He'd finished eating and he'd finished

looking at her scrapbook and listening to her point of view. She had only one weapon left in her arsenal. Slipping away, she hurried back to the kitchen where she pulled a large portion of a beautiful tiramisu out of the refrigerator. Rummaging in a drawer, she found a candle, which she lit and put atop it. She smiled with satisfaction, then carried it back out into the dining room, singing *"Tanti auguri a te,"* as she went. She stopped, put the blazing pastry down before him, and added, *"Buon compleanno!"*

He was laughing again, only this time it was with her, not at her.

"How did you know it was my birthday?" he asked her, letting her see, for just a moment, how pleased he was.

She shrugged grandly. "You told me."

He frowned. "When?"

"It was the first thing you said when you came into the kitchen, before you realized it was me instead of Renzo."

"Oh, of course."

He looked into the flame as though it fascinated him. She watched him. In the afternoon light, his scar looked like a ribbon of silver across his face. She wondered if it gave him any pain. She knew it gave him heartache. And because of that, it gave her heartache, too.

"Make a wish and blow out the candle," she told him.

He looked at her and almost smiled. "What shall I wish for?"

She shook her head. "It's your wish. And don't tell me, or else it won't come true."

His face took on a hint of an attitude, teasing her. "Okay. I know what I'm going to wish for."

She knew he didn't mean anything by it; still, the implication was there, hovering in the air between them. She felt herself flushing and turned away, biting her lip.

"Go ahead. Blow it out. I won't watch."

"Why not?" He blew out the small fire and picked up a fork. "Anyone can watch. It's not much of an event, you know."

He broke off a bit of the pastry onto his fork, and, instead of taking the bite himself, he waited until she'd turned back and then popped it between her lips and left it there.

"Hey!" She ate it quickly, half laughing. "That was for you. I ate enough of it myself when I was making the thing."

He stopped, staring at her. The tiramisu was a thing of beauty, the dark of the coffee flavor and the cocoa topping a striking contrast to the light-as-a-feather, rich, creamy layers. It was a mystery to him how anyone made such a thing, and the thought that she had created it on her own was a revelation. Her talents were legion, it seemed.

"You made it yourself?"

She nodded. Yes, she had, thinking of him the whole time and warding off Susa, who'd wanted to take over.

Max shook his head as he studied her face, searching her eyes, sketching a trail of interest along the line of her chin. "You made me that delicious pasta and you made me my birthday dessert with your own hands." His eyes seemed to glow with a special light and his voice was so quiet, she could hardly hear him. "What can I do for you in return, Isabella?"

She met his gaze and held it. "You know what I want," she said, almost as softly as he had spoken.

He stared into her eyes a moment longer, then his face took on an expression she couldn't translate into anything but regret. Looking down, he began to eat and he didn't speak again until he had finished.

"Thank you," he said simply. "I appreciate this."

She waited. Was he going to relent? Was he going to

tell her she could have another try at his hillside? She waited another moment, but he didn't seem to have anything else to say, so she sighed and rose, beginning to clear the plates away.

"I suppose I'd better get all this cleaned up," she said, wondering if she'd actually made any impression on him at all. "I'm sure you have people coming over to help you celebrate tonight."

He looked up at her with a frown. "I don't see visitors. Not ever. I thought you understood that."

She stopped, staring at him. "Not anyone?"

"No. Not anyone."

Her blue eyes betrayed her bewilderment. "Why not?"

He sighed and threw down his napkin, then said in a clipped tone, "I think that's self-evident."

She sank back into her chair and gaped at him. She remembered suddenly what Susa had said about his having lost his young wife years ago. She'd implied that the pain of losing her had brought on his lonely existence, but surely there was more to it than that. "You mean, because of your face?"

He merely stared at her, confirming her suspicions.

"But…" She choked, unable to comprehend his motives. "Why would you let something like that ruin your life? You need people around you, you need…"

She stopped before she said something ill-advised. He needed love. That much was obvious. He needed a woman, someone to care for him and make him happy. Every man needed that.

But did she have any business saying such a thing? Of course not. Especially since she needed a man just as badly, and look how she'd been unable to take care of that little problem for years now. She didn't even have the excuses he had. So who was she to talk?

But she couldn't leave the subject alone.

"If I were like you," she said, pointing to her own injured eye, "I would have hidden myself away and we would have had to close down the restaurant for the last week and a half."

He half smiled at her characterization and he looked at her black eye almost affectionately.

"Did you get any reaction from your customers?"

"Of course." She stared at him again. He was a prince, rich and probably famous in certain circles, powerful, with resources she could only dream of. So how had he let this happen? How had others around him let it go this far? How had he become such a recluse, and how could he stand it for so long?

"I get plenty of reaction," she continued slowly, "lots of double takes, people turning back to have another look at me. Then I get the opposite, people who notice, then look away quickly as though thinking I must have been beaten up and would be embarrassed if they acknowledged seeing the evidence of it."

He nodded, recognizing the experience from his own ventures out into the world.

"I even have little children making fun of me in the street." She tossed her hair back with a defiant snap of her head. "But who cares? That's their problem."

He gazed at her in complete admiration. She was a tough one. She could handle what life threw at her in ways he didn't seem capable of. But there was so much more to his situation that she didn't know about. "Our conditions are not comparable," he said.

She shook her head. "Maybe not to the degree, but the basics are very much the same."

He frowned, beginning to feel a bit of backlash against

her attitude. "You don't understand." He glanced at her, then away. "You don't know why this happened."

She leaned forward, her elbow on the table, her chin in her hand, ready to hear, ready to understand. "So tell me."

His gaze darkened. For just a moment he saw it all again, the trees rushing past his window, the huge old bridge standing right in his path, the flash as they hit, the flames, the fire, the horrible sound of metal against concrete. They said no one should have lived through that crash. And there were times when he'd cursed his own powers of survival.

Looking up, he spoke dismissively. "No."

Her eyes widened. "Why not?"

His own eyes were as cold as they'd ever been as he turned to gaze at her again. "It's none of your business."

He was right, of course, but she drew back as though he'd slapped her.

"Oh."

She rose again and turned toward the door. He'd hurt her with those words, with that manner. She'd thought they were becoming friends and he'd shown her just how far from that they really were. She was not allowed into his real life. Of course, what had she expected? This was a cold, cruel world, after all.

"I'll just get out of your way, then," she said stiffly. She walked firmly out of the room, waiting at each step for him to call her back. But he didn't say a word.

It only took her a few minutes to get her things washed up and ready to go, but she banged the pots a bit more than necessary. She was angry. There was no denying it. After all she'd done, all she'd said, and he still didn't understand!

She was packing her supplies away in her backpack when he came into the kitchen again. She looked up hopefully, but his eyes were still cold as ice.

"Where did you park your car?" he asked.

She went back to putting her full attention on what she was doing, stuffing the last of her utensils into the bag. "Don't worry about me. I can take care of myself."

He erased the distance between them and took her chin in his hand, forcing her to look up at him. "I've told you I won't have you wandering around the grounds on your own," he reminded her sternly. "I'll drive you to your car."

A captive, she stared back at him without saying anything. She wasn't fooled. He wanted to see where it was that she was sneaking in. Good thing she'd parked a distance away from the chink in the wall. If he was going to find her secret, he was going to have to survey the wall himself, brick by brick.

"I'll do fine on my own," she said again.

"I'm going to drive you. I brought my car around while you were cleaning up."

Slowly, deliberately, she pushed his hand away from her chin. "If you insist," she said coldly.

His mouth twitched, but he managed not to smile at the fierce picture she made.

"I do," he responded. "Shall we go?"

He helped her carry her things outside and there was a slinky little BMW Roadster.

"Nice car," she allowed, refusing to meet his gaze.

"It's a beauty, isn't it?" he agreed, stowing her things behind the seat and holding the door for her. "It seems like something of a waste. I almost never get to drive it."

"Why not?"

He shrugged. "The only place I go is to my home on the coast, and I travel in a limousine for that."

"With darkened windows. I know." Susa had told her all about it. "All so others won't see your face?" she asked, troubled by such a denial of life.

"There's more to it than that," he said, sliding behind the wheel.

"Of course. And it's none of my business." She stared out the side window.

He twitched and gave her a look, then started the car and eased it out onto the driveway.

"I don't know why you think you should be let in on every little aspect of my interior life," he said gruffly. "Believe me, the nuances are not all that interesting."

She whipped her head around. "I didn't ask just because I was snoopy," she said indignantly. "I actually care—" she stopped dead, realizing what she was saying "—uh...about you," she ended softly and lamely, looking away again as quickly as she could.

He didn't answer. As they cruised down the two-lane road he wondered why her admitting that she cared sent warmth careening through his system. It wasn't as though women hadn't cared for him in the past. What made her so special?

"Is that your car?" he asked as they closed in on a silver-blue compact sitting by the side of the road.

"That's it," she admitted.

He pulled up behind it and frowned as he studied the wall of his own property. "This isn't where you go in," he noted.

She flashed him a triumphant smile.

"You're right. This isn't it."

She began to gather her things for her great escape, slipping out of the Roadster and reaching for her bag before he had a chance to get out and help her.

"Bye," she said, not meeting his gaze and turning for her car.

"Hey." He got out on his side and followed her. "Wait a minute."

Throwing her bags into the backseat of her car, she

turned to look at him, though she was poised to jump behind the wheel and race off.

"What is it?" she asked guardedly.

He stood facing her, his legs wide apart, his hands hooked on the belt of his jeans. For a moment, he seemed lost in the depths of her eyes. Then he shrugged and looked almost bored with it all.

"I think I've come up with a way for you to get your precious herb," he said casually.

Her jaw dropped and her eyes opened wide. "What? How?"

"It's simple really."

"You mean you'll trust me to go alone?"

Darkness flashed across his face.

"No, of course not. I've told you, I will not allow you to go there unattended."

"Unattended?" Her frustration was plain on her face. She obviously felt they were just going around in circles. "But who would be available to go with me?"

He shrugged, his head cocked at a rather arrogant angle. "I'll do it," he said.

For just a moment, she wasn't sure she'd heard him correctly. "What?" she said. But she could tell he meant what he'd said by the look on his face. Joy swept through her. "You!" And then spontaneous happiness catapulted her right up against his chest.

"Oh, thank you, thank you!" she cried, throwing her arms around his neck and kissing his cheek again and again. "Thank you so much!"

He laughed softly, holding her loosely, resisting the impulse to take advantage of her giddiness.

"Can we go right now?" she cried, looking as though she could fly all the way on her own.

"Today it's too late," he said sensibly. "Come tomorrow."

"Yes." She knew he was right. "Yes, I will."

He stroked her temple with his forefinger, smoothing back the tiny curls that were forming at her hairline. "And when you come tomorrow, you can drive in the front gate."

She stared at him, clutching his arm. "How am I going to do that?"

"I'll give you the code."

That took her breath away. "Why would you do a thing like that?"

His gaze was cool, yet intimate. "Why not? I trust you." For now, it suited him that she have the code, and that was that. He gave her a quick, quirky smile.

"Besides, I can change the code any time I decide I don't want you to have it any longer."

There were tears in her eyes. She'd been so downhearted and now she was so happy. "Why are you being so good to me?" she asked emotionally.

His smile faded. He gazed deeply into her eyes and winced a bit from what he saw there. And then, he told her the truth.

"Because I care about you, too," he said.

CHAPTER SEVEN

"You've been to see the prince again." Susa's tone was quietly jubilant, as though she'd just won a bet.

Isabella turned and glanced at her sideways. "How did you know?"

Susa smiled and looked superior, mixing gelatin into the whipping cream as a stiffener, preparing for the fabulous desserts she would be concocting that evening. Very casually, she shrugged.

"I know many things."

Susa was like a member of the family. After Isabella's mother died, it was Susa she often turned to for those familiar motherly things that she needed. It was Susa who taught her how to act with the customers, how to say, "Please," and, "Thank you," and look as if you meant it. When Luca was putting her into jeans and plaid shirts as though she were a little boy, Susa taught her how to wear frilly dresses. She had a lot to thank the woman for. But Susa could be annoying, all the same.

Just like family.

Her silver hair was set in neat curls around her head, augmented by tortoiseshell combs. She looked ageless and infinitely efficient, which was just exactly what she was.

Looking at her, Isabella had a flash of appreciation for the woman. Without her, they couldn't run this restaurant these days. If nothing else, she was completely loyal. And very good at making pastries.

Isabella stared at her for a long moment, then sighed. "Someone told you, didn't they? Someone who saw me driving up there."

"Perhaps. Or perhaps I saw it myself." She threw out a significant look. "I've told you before, I have the gift."

Isabella rolled her eyes, turning back to her garlic press.

"I just want to warn you to be careful," Susa said after a long pause."

Isabella nodded. "Everyone is warning me to be careful."

"You need a warning." Susa looked up sharply. "You're reckless. You trust people too much and you get hurt."

Isabella tried to keep her temper. "I also eat too many sweets and stay up too late watching old movies. We should put up a chart with all my vices on it, so everyone can see."

It was Susa's turn to roll her eyes and Isabella bit her lip, regretting that she'd spoken sharply.

But the woman wasn't chastened. "Just a word to the wise," she said crisply. "In the first place, stay away from the prince. But if you must go to see him, stay away from water." She got up from her seat and headed for the washroom.

Isabella stared after her, then jumped up and followed her to the door.

"What are you talking about?" she demanded.

"Oh, nothing." Susa disappeared into the washroom.

"Susa!"

Isabella began to pace impatiently, waiting for her to return. Whatever she was hinting at, she had to know her reasons. There was no doubt something was still bothering Max about his wife's death. And there was no doubt

he was overly worried about that river. She would see how much Susa knew—or thought she knew—and then try to find out the truth on her own.

Susa came back out, smiling happily, knowing she had rocked Isabella's world.

"Well?" Isabella demanded. "Tell me what you mean by that water crack."

Susa shrugged. "That was how his young wife died. She drowned right in front of him."

"What?" Isabella suddenly felt breathless. "Why don't I know about this?"

"The family kept it quiet." Susa touched her arm in something close to sympathy. "There were whispers, but no one knew for sure what had happened." She shook her head. "But signs were not good."

Isabella regained her equilibrium and frowned, beginning to get suspicious.

"Why would you know about this if nobody else does?"

"I told you." She pointed to her own temple. "The gift," she said, her eyes widening.

"Susa!"

She smiled like a cat with a secret. "And also, I know because my cousin was working there, up at the castle, at the time."

That put a little more credence behind it, Isabella had to admit. Susa seemed to have relatives working everywhere. Isabella shook her head. She supposed that was all a part of having "the gift."

"So tell me everything you heard," she demanded.

Susa shrugged, starting toward the refrigerator. "I know she drowned in the river, right there on the estate. The two of them were there alone. There are those who think…" She raised her eyebrow significantly.

"No!" Isabella cried. She was furious, but she had a deep, sinking feeling in the pit of her stomach all the same. "I don't believe that for a minute."

Susa shrugged. "You never know."

But Isabella knew very well that Max could never have hurt anyone. Could he? Of course not. It was inconceivable.

Susa had no more information, but she'd said enough to send Isabella into orbit. This news was all she could think about. Her heart thumped as she went over this possibility and that probability. She wanted to run to Max, to see if he knew about these rumors. But how could she bring something like this up? Impossible. And she knew without a doubt that he wouldn't want to hear a word about it.

Still, it made her crazy to think of people suspecting him. She ached with it, wanting to defend him even though...

Even though she didn't even know if anything Susa said was real or just wild imaginings in the woman's mind. Slowly, she calmed herself. There was really no point in letting herself get so worked up when she didn't even know if any of this was true.

She looked at the clock. In just eighteen hours, she would see him again. Thinking about it, she felt a strange tingling spread from her chest down her arms to her fingertips, and that was when she knew she was letting herself make too much of this—and it was time to come back to earth.

The whole thing was a mistake and Max knew it. Sitting in his darkened library, he sipped from his third glass of aged port and pondered what he was going to do about it. A wood fire flickered in the stone fireplace. The huge old house creaked with its antiquity and echoed with its emptiness. He was alone—just the way he wanted it to be.

So what had he been thinking when he'd told Isabella

she could come back here? He knew very well her presence would begin to eat away at everything he thought he'd settled years ago. He needed to be alone. He didn't deserve anything else. What he'd done when he'd allowed his wife and the baby she was carrying to die in the river was an unforgivable crime. He would never be able to pay off that debt. It would take the rest of his life just to begin paying.

Closing his eyes, he fought back the doubt that had begun to tease him lately. He'd been sure all along that his scarred face was a judgement of fate, that it was a part of his punishment, that it helped to keep him in the private prison where it was fitting and appropriate that he be. For years he'd been—not content, exactly, but resigned.

Now Isabella had fallen into his life and that was a temptation in itself. He wanted her. He wanted to be with her. He wanted to be happy.

Was it really so wrong to want that? Could he resist all that Isabella had to offer him and his life?

"Laura," he murmured, shaking his head. "Oh, Laura."

If only he could feel that she was still there with him, he knew he could be stronger. As it was, he was going to have to count on his own sense of honor.

"Honor," he muttered darkly, and then an ugly, obscene word came out of his mouth and anger boiled up inside him. Filled with a surge of rage, he threw the glass against the fireplace. It smashed into a hundred pieces with a satisfying crunch. Watching the broken shards of glass fly through the air, he felt his anger dissipate just as quickly.

He could only do what he could do, but he would resist. That was the life he had made for himself. He was stuck with it.

* * *

Max was waiting for Isabella as she drove up to the front entry of the old castle. She assumed he'd been warned by a signal from the gate she'd had no trouble opening with the code he'd given her. His shoulders looked incredibly wide in a crisp, open-necked blue shirt. His smooth-fitting chinos accentuated his athletic form, giving her a tiny bubble of appreciative happiness for just a moment. But something about his stance and the way his arms were folded across his chest told her he was bound and determined to get the two of them back on a cool, polite trajectory and away from all the warmth they'd managed to generate between them the day before.

Uh oh, she thought as she slid from behind the wheel, her heart beating a little faster.

Surely he wasn't going to change his mind about the basil. She gave him a tentative glance, then reached into the backseat to get the basket of sandwiches she'd made for the trip to the hillside. Before she could turn with it, he was there, shaking his head.

"How did I know you would bring a picnic lunch?" he said wryly. "Better leave it here. I don't think it's a good idea."

She looked at him blankly, clutching her basket and not sure what the problem was.

"This isn't an outing, Isabella," he said coolly, his dark eyes shadowed. "It's a job to be done. Let's get on with it."

"But, the sandwiches won't keep out here in the sun and—"

"Give your basket to Renzo," he said.

She turned, surprised to see that the older man was standing there with his hand outstretched. Gingerly, she handed him her basket and tried a small smile. The man gave her a small smile back, and that helped a bit.

Turning, Max began to stride toward a fence that ran along part of the long driveway where two horses were saddled and ready to go. She hurried to follow him.

"You do know how to ride, don't you?" he asked over his shoulder.

Did she? She swallowed, looking at how big both beasts were.

"I've been riding a time or two," she admitted reluctantly, remembering one successful trip around the lake and another painful excursion in the mountains when she was younger.

But she was pretty sure she could do it. Given a choice, she would rather have walked with him all the way. But he was obviously in a hurry today. That was disappointing. But at least the trip was still on. She ought to be grateful for that.

"Don't worry, Mimi is gentle as a lamb," he told her, reaching out to stroke the downy nose of a gray mare with a black, silky mane. "She'll treat you right." His face softened as the horse nuzzled into the palm of his hand with clear affection. "Won't you, girl?"

Isabella watched, surprised to see him show such open emotion so effortlessly. That made her wonder what he'd been like before the accident that had scarred him. Had he been happy? Carefree? Had affection come naturally to him? Somehow she thought so. What a blessing it would be if somehow she could help him get that life back.

She bit her lip, knowing how ridiculous that thought was. She had no business thinking it. His life had nothing to do with her. Hadn't he even told her so? But as she watched him gently stroke the beautiful horse, she found herself wondering if the touch of his hand was as gentle when he stroked a woman, and she flushed.

And then it came to her in a flash of intuition—this had

been his wife's horse. Of course. And that made her even more nervous about riding.

But the mounting went fine and soon they were trotting slowly out of the yard and onto the fields of the estate, she on Mimi and Max on the stunning black stallion he had been riding the night they'd met. Very quickly, she began to feel at ease, as though she were an experienced rider herself. Mimi was the perfect mount for a greenhorn such as she was.

The day was gorgeous, bright and breezy and full of promise. They were riding over territory she'd never been through before, rolling hills and green meadows. And then they came over a rise and below them spread an ancient vineyard with grape stakes as far as she could see.

She pulled the horse to a stop and made an exclamation of surprise as she looked at the limitless plain of struggling grape plants.

"What is this?" she asked him.

He leaned forward in the saddle and gazed at the expanse of it with one hand shading his eyes.

"This was once the Rossi vineyard," he said, his voice even and emotionless. "It supplied grapes for our small family winery, an enterprise that lasted for a couple of hundred years." He paused, then added dispassionately, "It was abandoned almost ten years ago."

"Abandoned? Why?"

He didn't turn to meet her gaze, and for a long moment, he didn't answer. Watching him, she suddenly realized his neck was strained, as though he were holding something back, something painful. Her breath caught in her throat. She wanted to reach out to him, to touch him, but she didn't dare. So she waited, and finally he spoke.

"I'm sure you know that I was married when I was younger. And that my...my wife died." His voice almost

choked, but he went on firmly. "At the time it happened, everything stopped. Life stopped."

Turning, he stared into her eyes as though he was forcing himself to do it. "I mean that literally. All the workers were sent away, except a bare skeleton crew to keep the place from completely reverting to the wild." His eyes seemed to burn. "And I've never seen a good reason to bring any of them back." He stared at her a moment longer, then looked away. "It's better this way."

She shook her head. *Better for whom?* she wanted to say. But who was she to tell him how to live his life?

"It seems so lonely," was all she dared put out. "And such a waste."

He shrugged again. "There are plenty of vineyards in Italy," he said, giving his horse a snicker that started him moving again. "One more or less won't make a difference."

She sighed. So he thought she was talking about his grape plants? Well, maybe she was. But she'd meant a lot more than that. A waste, indeed.

They crested another hill and found a small forest barely protecting a group of small stone buildings.

"What's that?" she called to him, pointing at it.

He turned and looked, then grinned at her. "The family crypt," he said. "Want to see it?"

"Oh! Yes."

He helped her dismount and they tied the horses to a gate, then walked slowly into the little glen that held his ancestors' graves. The garden was overgrown, but not completely shabby. His caretaker had kept it decent, if not pristine. There was a small pond with tiny flashing fishes darting back and forth, a rose garden and a marble chapel. And behind them all was a larger, brooding stone building

that had served as a mausoleum to the Rossi family through the Middle Ages and beyond.

Isabella loved it. The place seemed like a secret, enchanted garden, full of history and family stories. But what was most stunning to her as she rounded a corner was a life-size marble statue of a half-naked man with a sword held at the ready guarding the entrance. Carved at the base of the marble was the name Adonis Salviati Di Rossi, 1732-1801.

Isabella gasped, hands to her mouth, then whirled to face Max, who was right behind her.

"It looks just like you!" she cried.

He tried to keep a solemn face and raised one eyebrow cynically, but his pleased sense of humor was hard to hide. It shone from his dark eyes and along the lines that framed his wide mouth. This statue had been a source of teasing and torture for him in his younger days. His friends and cousins had called him "Adonis" and joked about reincarnation and ghostly presences. In fact, Isabella hadn't been the first to call him a vampire. His childhood playmates had done it as well.

He'd forgotten how much he hated it then. Now, it just seemed amusing.

"How would you know?" he challenged her. "You're not really sure what I look like at all."

"Oh, yes," she said, no doubt in her mind. "I know exactly what you look like."

She said it with such firm confidence, he looked at her, bemused. He felt so comfortable around her. Whenever he looked into her eyes, all he saw was a candid sort of joy in life. He hadn't believed her when she'd first told him she didn't see him as ugly. But ever since, he hadn't been able to detect one sign of anything negative in her eyes, and he'd definitely been looking for it.

Still, he had to remember that she represented nothing but peril to him. She appealed to him, emotionally, physically, temperamentally—in every way possible. He wanted to be with her. He wanted to hear her laugh. He wanted to feel her in his arms. There was no denying the fact that she made him happy—happier than he'd been in years.

Happier than he had any right to be.

And that was the danger. He had no business dragging her into his private limbo of a life. He would do what he could to help her with her herbal requirements, but that was all. Once he had her supplied, she would be on her way and he wouldn't see her again. Ever again.

At least that was the way he'd planned it. Now that she was here with him, it seemed almost impossible to think of losing her. She filled a need and a hunger in him he hadn't even realized he still had.

And so, she was dangerous.

He followed as she explored the mausoleum, chattering happily as she looked into everything, finding all she saw wonderful and interesting. And he wished...

But what the hell was the point of wishing? The more you wanted out of life, the less you got. He was through with wishing. There was a job to be done here and that was all he was prepared to do.

Over and out.

Isabella knew she was talking too much, but she couldn't help it. The day was so nice and the man she was with was so mesmerizing, she was bubbling with joy just being with him.

And yet, she knew he was troubled. She could sense it in his silence and in the look in his dark eyes. As they got

back atop their horses and began the last leg of their trip to the hillside, she ached to help him, if only she knew how.

But that was silly, wasn't it? He had everything he might want; all he had to do was order it up and it would be there for him. What could she provide that he couldn't get on his own?

Right behind them in the little courtyard was the evidence of a life that was one of a long line of important people involved in important events. Ordinary people such as she was didn't find their ancestors memorialized in tombs like this. Here was history, a background to the story of her area. She was a spectator. He was a star of the show.

"What's it like being an Italian prince?" she asked him at one point.

He shrugged and gave her a look. "You know very well it's an honorary title these days. The monarchy was abolished in 1946."

"But you're still a prince. You still have a special place in history."

"Bah," was all he would say.

She smiled. The fact that her own father had been a part, though small, of that background was fascinating to her. She'd wanted to ask her father about his visits to the palazzo in the old days from the moment she'd got home from her visit to Max the day before.

For some reason, she still hadn't told him that she'd met the prince. She wasn't sure why she was hesitating, but something told her he wouldn't necessarily be pleased. So her approach was less direct than usual.

She'd found her father trying to practice using a walker and she'd watched for a while, giving him advice as he'd grown more and more impatient. His ex-friend Fredo had been to see him again and put him in a rotten mood.

"Now he's threatening me with health violations," he grumbled. "Me! I've always had the cleanest kitchen in the village. And yet he dares to call me a violator!"

She got him calmed down and made him sit in his chair to rest, then brought him a cold lemonade and perched next to him, ready for the inquisition.

"Papa, tell me," she said, trying to sound casual. "How did you first know about the *Monta Rosa Basil*? When did you first find it?"

He sat back and slowly he lost the tense look around his eyes as he went into the past with a dreamy look on his face.

"As it happened, I was catering a picnic for the old prince, Prince Bartholomew, and his family, on the top of the hill, just above where the basil grows. I did more catering on my own in those days. I took every side job I could just to keep afloat. Money was very tight. There was hardly enough income to keep my stand going and I had to make some painful sacrifices just to survive." She nodded encouragement, though at the same time she wondered if he didn't see that they were close to being in that position again right now.

"There was a young maid who worked for the prince's family. She showed me the herb. Made me pay a forfeit for some silliness or other by eating a leaf. I put it on my tongue, and I immediately knew it was something I'd never tasted before. At first I thought it strange. But I couldn't get that taste out of my mind."

Isabella nodded. Everyone was the same, instantly in love with the magic.

"So the next time I was on the grounds, I went to that hill again and picked some of the herb, took it home and tried it in some recipes." He snapped his fingers in the air. "Instant success. Everyone loved it."

How exciting that must have been for him. She smiled, loving him. Growing up without a mother, she'd always felt extra close to her father. His happiness was hers, sometimes too much so.

"Did they have a lot of parties in those days?" she asked, curious to know everything she could about Max's upbringing.

"Yes. Whole caravans of people would come from Rome or from Naples and stay a week."

She shook her head with wonder. "Why don't I remember any of this?"

"These things ended when you were a young child." Luca sighed. "After Prince Bartholomew's beautiful wife killed herself, the parties never resumed. In fact, he began to spend all his time in Rome after that."

"Killed herself!" She sat up straighter and stared at her father. He had to be talking about Max's mother. An icy hand gripped her heart. "What happened?"

"I don't know the details. They said she jumped from a balcony." He shook his head. "Poor thing. She was a film star, you know. She worked with Fellini and Antonioni. She was quite good. It was a tragedy."

What a series of tragedies in Max's family if all these stories were true. First his mother commited suicide, then his young wife drowned. And what about his own accident, the one that had done such damage to his face? She still didn't have the details on that.

It was no wonder he had troubled eyes as they rode across his estate lands. He'd come by them naturally, it seemed. She looked over at him now and found him looking back at her.

"Just a little further," he called to her from the back of his horse.

She nodded. "Your grounds are so beautiful. You should do something with them."

He looked out over his hills. "You think so? What do you suggest?"

She wanted to throw out her arms to encompass it all. "I don't know. You should share this with the world. Maybe put in a hotel, a spa, a destination resort."

He turned to look at her again, grinning. "Isabella, what a middle-class mind you have. Must everything make you money?"

"No, but…"

She flushed, realizing he was teasing her, and she dropped her defensiveness and returned to a light-hearted mode.

"Hey, it's the money-making middle class that makes the economy hum for everyone," she reminded him. "Let's have none of your upper-class arrogance."

"The idle rich," he muttered dismissively.

"Exactly."

But she was laughing.

"You think I'm lazy, don't you?" he said, as though it was a revelation to him.

"Not at all. I just think you don't have an eye out for profit. The spice of life."

He shook his head. His eyes were warm. For the moment, his troubled look had faded. "Tell me this, Isabella," he said. "You've said your restaurant was in trouble because you couldn't get the best ingredients. Is this going to make that big a difference? Will all be well now?"

She hesitated, tempted to fudge the truth a little. This was such a subject of frustration for her. But when she looked at his face, she knew she could never be less than frank with him.

"No," she said simply. "All will not be well. My father

is a wonderful man and a good cook, but he can't run a business to save his life. We are in big trouble financially, and in all sorts of other ways. I'm not sure we'll last much longer no matter how much good food we cook up."

He nodded. From what she'd told him and a few things he'd heard from Renzo, he'd had a feeling that was the case.

"Maybe your father should let you take the reins," he said dryly. "You are the one who seems to have a passion for business."

That brought her up short, but she realized, very quickly, that he had a point. She had the instincts, though not the training. If only Luca would give her a chance…

"So what could I do to make a profit?" he asked her. "Besides turning my ancestral estate into a…what did you call it? A destination resort." He gave her a mock glare. "Something, by the way, that I would never do."

She took his question quite seriously. "Well, to begin with, you could renovate your vineyards. How about that? Wine sells very well these days."

He was laughing at her. It was obvious he wasn't taking this as seriously as she was. "Isabella, Isabella, what about the nobility of the grape?"

She made a face. "Nobility is a pose," she said. "Something that looks nice for special occasions, but is shed in a moment when it's no longer working for you."

He threw back his head and laughed aloud. "I can see you have big plans for me. What in particular?"

"I was thinking after seeing your abandoned vine-yard…" She hesitated. Did she really want to tell him her thoughts? But why not? If not now, when?

"Well, you could hire my friend Giancarlo. The way some people restore businesses that have been run badly,

he restores vineyards. I'm sure he can get you up and running in no time."

He gazed at her as though he wasn't sure just how seriously to take what she was saying. "So I can sell my grapes?"

"Why not? Or how about your own winery? With a tasting room? Then you could run tours from the village. People love to tour wineries. A little wine tasting, a small bistro on the premises…"

He was laughing at her but she didn't care. "You could run my restaurant," he said with a grin.

"Thank you." She made a pretend curtsy from the saddle. "I'd love to."

What a great idea. She fairly shivered with excitement over it. To think of running a restaurant for Max! Of making the special sauce for tourists who would come from far and wide…

But she quickly brought herself back down to earth. It was a pipe dream and she knew it. He refused to come face-to-face with strangers. He wouldn't even let vineyard workers on his land. How could he stand to have tourists? It wasn't going to happen.

They crested another hill and there below them was the field where the basil grew. She leaned forward in the saddle and sighed with relief. She'd had a dream during the night that she'd arrived here only to find the earth scorched and not a plant in sight. At least that hadn't happened.

But that dream had cast a pall on her morning. She'd thought of it with dread as she was preparing the picnic lunch to take with her. Was it a sign? Should she be prepared for the worst?

Susa had raised an eyebrow at the preparations, but didn't say a thing. Isabella ignored her and packed sandwiches in a basket and stowed them in her little car.

"Where are you going?" her father called from the doorway.

She hesitated. Should she tell him? Dashing back to give him a hug, she whispered in his ear, "I think I will have the basil with me when I return. Say a prayer for me." And she kissed his leathery cheek, turned and hurried off before he had time to question her further.

And all the time, she'd wondered if the basil would even be there once she made her way to it. Now she knew. It was here all right. And she was going to take as much of it as she could.

CHAPTER EIGHT

ISABELLA slid down off the horse and began to collect the basil, snipping leaves with little scissors she'd brought along with her. Max dismounted as well, but he stood back, watching her, and when she glanced up she noticed that all his good humor had fled. In fact, he looked ill at ease.

This was the place he considered too dangerous to let her visit alone, but she still couldn't really understand why. The hillside looked quite benign. The river was racing past below, and she knew how he felt about the river, but even if she started to slide there were plenty of places where she would be able to break her fall. No, she didn't get it. The place seemed fine to her.

The only problem was, the basil was not quite at its peak and there was only a limited amount she could harvest at the moment. She was going to have to discuss this with him and ask to come again in a week or so. Was he going to allow it? She had no idea.

It did seem all his warmth had evaporated and all he wanted to do was hurry up and get her to finish up and head for home again. Looking at his face, she decided to deal with her problem later.

"Okay," she told him at last, tying her two large bags together. "I think I have enough for now."

He nodded, handing her Mimi's reins and helping her aboard, then turning to mount his own horse. Isabella turned to look at him, and as she did the reins slipped from her hand.

"Oh!" She started to lean down to get them again, but the bags full of basil began to fall and she had to grab for them instead, stuffing them under a strap to hold them tightly secure.

And in that moment, something went wrong. She was never able to pinpoint exactly what happened, but something frightened the sweet, gentle horse who had been so pleasant all day, and suddenly she turned into a different animal.

"Max!" Isabella cried, grabbing handfuls of mane in order to keep from falling. "Stop her!"

Mimi wasn't waiting around to see what Max would do. She neighed in an alarming way and shot off toward the river.

"Max!"

Isabella hung on for dear life. The water was straight ahead.

"No, Mimi!" she cried, seeing another dunking in her future, at the very least. Closer and closer—the river looked inevitable. Then, suddenly Mimi veered away, racing along the bank, into the trees.

In a moment, a small clearing appeared, and a beautiful waterfall, and Mimi came to an abrupt stop. Too abrupt. Isabella sailed right over her head and landed in the brush. Mimi seemed to understand exactly what she'd done and decided not to stick around and find out what her punishment would be. Instead, she took off again, this time with an empty saddle.

Isabella moaned, pulling herself out of the brambles and seeing Max arrive just too late.

"At least I didn't get wet this time," she commented shakily, then stopped dead as she saw Max's ashen face. He leaped from his horse and grabbed her, looking her over as though he expected to find broken limbs and gaping flesh wounds.

"Are you all right?" he demanded harshly. "Isabella, are you okay?"

"I'm fine. I think." After all, she hadn't had time to take an inventory. "I'm okay, but poor Mimi…"

He swore in a way that would have sent chills down Mimi's spine if she'd heard him. "Never mind that damn horse. You could have been killed."

"But I wasn't."

"No, but…" He took her by the shoulders, searching her face, then looked over his shoulder at the waterfall with such a look of dread, it took her breath away.

"What is it, Max?"

She put her hands flat against his chest, staring into his face. And suddenly, she knew.

"Is this where…?"

He looked at her as though he'd never seen her before.

"We have to go," he said curtly. "We have to get out of here."

"Oh, Max."

He turned toward the horse and swung up, pulling her up in front of him just as he had that first night. His face was like stone but she could feel the tension in him and see it in the cords of his neck. His dark eyes were filled with pain and a pulse was beating at his temple. She saw all this and didn't dare say a word. Just before they started off, he looked back toward the waterfall and the anguish in his face sent her reeling. Here, obviously, was the core and crux of his torment. This had to be the place where his young wife had died.

They rode hard back toward the palazzo, but after a few minutes the horse swerved into another direction and she realized he was taking them to the Rossi cemetery instead. They arrived and he lowered her, then dismounted himself. Without a word, he turned and strode off into the courtyard. Biting her lip, she followed, though she wasn't at all sure she was welcome.

At first she thought he was heading for the little marble chapel, but he turned into the flower garden instead. Turning, he waited while she joined him. Her heart beat like a drum as she looked into the desolation in his eyes.

"Isabella, I'm sorry. I…I think you've probably guessed why I was upset near the waterfall. I just need a few minutes to unwind. If you could wait out by the chapel…"

"You want me to go and wait for you?"

"Yes. Please."

She was already shaking her head. "No," she said. "No, I won't go."

He stared at her as though he wasn't sure she understood. "Isabella…"

"Max." She grabbed his arm and looked up into his tortured face. "I think you should talk about it. I think you should tell me…"

"No." He pulled away from her touch. "I don't talk about this. Not to anyone."

"That's why you must," she insisted passionately.

He began to back away, but she wouldn't let him go. "Max, don't you see? You need to talk about it. You've probably been holding it all inside for ten years. You have to talk." Tears filled her eyes. Taking his arm again, she shook it, not sure what else she could do to convince him. "Tell me about her. What was she like?"

He stared down at her. "Laura?" he asked softly.

"Yes," she said. "Tell me about Laura."

He turned woodenly and slumped onto the garden bench. She slipped in beside him, taking his hand in hers.

"What did she look like?" she asked gently.

"An angel." His voice was gruff as gravel and he cleared his throat. "Blonde hair, light as a feather. And so fragile…" His voice broke.

Isabella squeezed his hand. "You loved her."

"Yes." He nodded. "I loved her from the moment I saw her." His voice was getting stronger. "She was good and kind and so very loving. Our life together was like a fairy tale. We were so happy."

Isabella nodded as he went on and on about his wonderful wife. His pain was clear in his voice and it was agony just to listen to him. But it was also good. She needed it, too. She wanted to understand him.

"When we found out we were going to have a baby," he said at last, "we thought life couldn't get any better."

A baby. Isabella blinked hard and looked away. She hadn't realized Laura was pregnant. That only made it all so much worse. Her heart already ached for him, now it broke in two.

"Our favorite place to have a picnic was by the waterfall," he was saying. "But we shouldn't have gone that day." His voice was almost a monotone now. "I'd been up most of the night before trying to solve a problem with the accountant. I was dead tired. But Laura had been planning a special celebration and I didn't want to disappoint her. So we went, and we toasted the baby that was on the way, and we ate Laura's special croissants that she had just learned how to make." His voice was suddenly choked. "And then we lay back on the blanket, wrapped in each other's arms. And the next thing I knew, I was opening my eyes and she was gone."

His hand was gripping hers tightly now, so tightly she could hardly stand it, but she didn't complain.

"I looked around. I couldn't imagine where she could have gone. And then I saw a bit of her dress floating in the water." A shudder went through him and he pulled his hand away from hers, leaning forward, his face in his hands. "I was in a frenzy. I pulled her from the water. Her foot had been stuck between two stones. I was so sure I could make her breathe again. I tried and tried. But it was too late. She was dead." His voice was harsh now, harsh and grating.

"Gone forever."

And then his shoulders began to shake and she knew he was releasing his grief at last.

He blamed himself. She'd seen it in his eyes, in every fiber of his being, as though despair and regret were all he knew. He blamed himself and it was so unfair. How could she get him to see that?

She stayed beside him, very quiet, until she could sense he would accept a bit of comfort, and then she touched his back, rubbing her hand softly up and down.

"I'm sorry," she murmured. "Oh, Max, I'm so sorry."

He rose slowly and turned toward her, his face ravaged. "Don't be sorry for me," he said coldly. "I don't deserve it. I let her die. I let them both die."

She gasped. "Max, how can you say that? You were asleep."

"Yes. Exactly. I was asleep. I should have…" His voice faded.

"See? You can't even say what you should have done. You couldn't help it. Accidents are called accidents because no one means for them to happen."

He was shaking his head, looking at her with haunted eyes. "I should have saved her."

She searched her mind for some way to get him to see this from another perspective. "Should your father have saved your mother when she jumped from the balcony?" she said a bit wildly, and then clamped her hand over her mouth, realizing she didn't know enough about the incident to use it this way.

But to her surprise, he didn't seem to notice that. He answered directly. "He couldn't have done anything. She was alone at home when it happened. How could he have stopped that?"

Isabella threw out her hands. "And Laura was alone when she went into the water. You weren't there. You were asleep." She shook his arm again. "Max, you couldn't help it. It's not your fault."

He looked doubtful, but she could tell he was beginning to mull that over. She shook her head.

"At least you talked about it," she said.

He gave her a sardonic look. "Quite the junior psychologist, aren't you?" he said, but there was no animosity in his voice. To his own surprise, he did feel better. Not much, but a little better. Maybe.

And she could see the truth in him, in his face, in his attitude. She was glad she'd risked everything on pushing him to talk. For now, it seemed to have worked out for him. There was so much guilt, so much self-doubt in his heart. And for her, there was so much new background that she knew about him. No matter what she learned, everything only made her regard for him grow. Her father and Susa were wrong. She was glad she hadn't stayed away from royalty after all.

There was just one thing that still nagged at her. She didn't know the details of the crash that had taken his face, the accident no one seemed to know anything about. That was still a mystery.

* * *

"You're going to have to ride with me again," he told her as he led in the stallion, and she nodded, thinking what a contrast this was to the other night in the dark.

"It's way past noon," she fretted. "Now don't you wish we'd brought the picnic I made?"

He nodded, feeling a touch of chagrin. Looking at her, he realized what a fool he'd been. He'd thought he could keep her at arm's length if he only tried hard enough. Now he knew that wasn't going to happen. Though he couldn't see how anything real and lasting between them could work out in the long run, for now, when she was near, he was going to live in the moment. No more pretending, especially to himself.

"I'm hungry as a wolf," he admitted.

She grinned up at him. "I have a solution to that. There's a place very near here we can get the most wonderful food."

"What are you talking about?" he asked suspiciously.

"Do you know the little stand by the reservoir? Where the Spanish family sells tapas?"

His face cleared. "Yes, I've driven past it."

"And you've never been tempted to stop?"

He half smiled down at her. Her lively interest in everything was contagious. "Actually, I have, but…"

She put a hand on his arm. "We're going there."

That was going a little far. "What? Who's going where?" He thought she understood he didn't do things like that.

"You and me. We're going to go have some of his delicious tapas. You'll thank me for this."

He stood where he was, shaking his head and looking stubborn. "Isabella, I don't think…"

"Oh, Max, please." She hung on his arm and looked adorably hungry. "It's just outside your walls. We'll go out the gate and we'll ride up and you can stay outside, under

the trees. I'll go in and order the food. There are tables along the water." She made her face even more appealing. "At this time of day, we'll probably be the only ones there. You won't have to come face-to-face with another soul. I'll do that part."

He was still frowning but she could see he was going to bend. "I don't know."

"Yes, you do." She gave him her most playful smile. "You know very well you need this. You want it." She pulled on his arm. "Come on."

He gave in. He couldn't help it. To do anything else would seem churlish right now. He helped her up in front of him on his horse and they made their way through the gate, to the outside of the estate. This was territory he hadn't traveled in years, except to rush past in his limousine. There was something freeing about just venturing this far beyond his own walls.

The tables on the rise above the river were completely empty. He sat at one of them and she went in, bringing out a wonderful collection of small, delicious items, including prawn croquetas and chopped pork empanadas and sautéed artichokes. Señor Ortega trailed behind her carrying two bottles of cold beer, and Max tensed, waiting for the man to react to his scars. Maybe Isabella had warned him, but he showed no sign of noticing a thing, chattering on in his Spanish-accented Italian about how they should come back tomorrow because he was planning to make the best tapas ever seen in these parts and if they didn't return, they would miss that.

He smiled and nodded at the man, who turned back to the little stand, still talking as he went.

"Señor Ortega is a friend of my father's," Isabella told

him comfortably. "Someday he'll have his own full-size restaurant, just like we do."

The food was wonderful and the beer was ice-cold. They ate and talked and even laughed a bit together as though they'd known each other forever. Whenever she stopped to think about it, Isabella felt a glow. She could hardly believe they seemed so good together. She'd never known a man like this before.

They finished up and walked the horse back to the estate gate.

"You see?" she told him. "That wasn't so bad. You need to get out more and be a part of this area. After all, this place is yours. Your ancestors owned all this land and developed the village originally, didn't they? You can't just walk away and pretend it has no connection to you."

He rolled his eyes and made a gesture with his hand meant to show that she talked too much, and she laughed.

They stopped while he used his code to open the gate. It creaked out of the way, giving them room to enter, and she looked up and down the length of what she could see of the long stucco wall.

"I can't believe you have this wall around your whole huge property," she said. "It must be miles and miles long."

"And it took years and years to build it. About four hundred of them."

She sighed, feeling the history and the romance of it all. "And now the wind and rain and everything else is working hard to tear it back down again," she noted wistfully.

"Yes." He steadied his horse and helped her mount. "Just like that Robert Frost poem about there being something that does not love a wall," he added as he came up behind her and settled her into a comfortable place in front of him. "Nature abhors a wall more than it does a vacuum."

She nodded, relaxing against him and feeling his arms come around her waist with a sense of warm pleasure. "Maybe you should work on tearing down some of your walls," she murmured.

He groaned. "How did I know you were going to go in that direction?"

"Because you know you need to do it."

His voice hardened a bit. "I'm not going to be lectured by you," he warned her carefully.

She caught her breath. She certainly didn't want to put him off, but, still, he needed to begin to live a real life, and if she didn't help him do that, what good was she to him?

"Oh?" she said, deciding to use a humorous tone to help defray resentment. "Then who *will* you let do the lecturing?"

"No one."

His voice was firm, but not angry, and she risked going on with it.

"You see? That's your problem right there. You need other people in your life. You need to be with others, talk to people, hear some new opinions on things, new experiences in life. You're alone too much."

He shrugged. "I have the Internet."

"The Internet!" She turned to try to look him in the face. "That's like interacting with robots."

"They're not robots." He actually sounded a bit offended that she would say such a thing. "They're real people on real computers. I'm not quite the hermit you think I am."

She shook her head. "You can't see the people, you can't judge their emotions. You can't see their truth."

"Truth," he scoffed.

"Real life is better," she insisted stubbornly.

He was silent for a moment, then he said, softly, "Real life can be painful."

She drew in her breath. "Yes." She wished she could turn and hug him. He was holding her, but loosely, impersonally. It was odd to be so close, and yet so far apart. "Pain is like rain. You need it to grow."

He made a sound that was derisive, but with a touch of amusement that let her know he wasn't taking offense to all her philosophizing.

"Too much rain floods out life," he said, making it sound as though he were trying to bring in his own words to live by to stand against hers. "What then?" he challenged her.

"Then we learn to tread water," she shot back.

He laughed softly. "Don't worry about me, Bella. This is my lot in life. I can handle it."

She loved that he'd used that affectionate nickname for her, but she wasn't sure she liked the way his thoughts were tending otherwise.

She didn't know what he meant. Was he expressing a fatalistic acceptance of his scars, or was he saying he could rise above that if he wished? She wanted to know, but she wasn't sure she wanted to ask him to explain. So she was silent for the rest of the ride back to the castle.

They found Mimi grazing peacefully in the yard outside the kitchen with only about half the basil left under the strap that held the bags. Her wild ride to get home again must have sprayed it across the landscape.

"What a shame," Max said, a smile in his eyes. "It looks like you'll have to come back tomorrow and do this all over again."

She turned to look at him. He reached out and touched her cheek with the palm of his hand. She covered his hand with her own as she searched his eyes.

"Shall I come back?" she asked him, wanting to make sure.

He nodded. "Yes," he said.

She smiled at him, thinking of all they had been through today, and her heart was full. There were no words she could use, not right now. So she did the only thing she could think of. And in that moment, she would have done anything for him.

Reaching up, she took his face between her hands and kissed his mouth. He started to pull away at first, but she didn't let him go. She kissed him and held him close and used her body to tell him what she couldn't say with words. In a moment, he responded, curling his arms around her and kissing her back.

When she finally drew back, her eyes were swimming with tears, but his were smiling.

"Isabella," he said softly, holding her chin in his hand as he looked into her eyes with something close to affection. "How did you so quickly become the sunshine of my life? Without you, I live in darkness. I only wish…"

He didn't say what he wished, but she thought she knew. He wished she were just a little different. He wished he were just a bit more free to act on his inclinations. She wished those things too, and her heart broke a little just because reality was so cruel. But, for now, she was happy just to be with him. It was all she needed.

Isabella's joy in the day faded quickly once she got back to the restaurant. Her father was waiting for her, his face creased with worry.

"Where have you been?" he demanded.

"I…Papa, I've brought back basil." She lifted the bag to show him. "We'll be able to use it again right away. I…"

"You've been with the prince." He said the words as though she'd destroyed herself and her family's reputation in one fell swoop and there was no turning back.

"What?"

She tried to laugh at his serious attitude. It was so completely over the top and something she'd never expected from him. But he was obviously sincere. This sort of anguish just floored her.

"Papa, it's all right. He's allowing me to continue to harvest the leaves and he's helping me…."

Luca waved away her explanations. "I've heard all about it. I know you've been seeing him. And we all know what that means."

Her head went back. She didn't deserve this. Anger shot through her veins. Here she'd practically turned her life inside out in order to get the desperately needed ingredient, and when she returned in triumph, no one cared.

"Yes, I've been seeing him," she retorted. "But I don't think it means what you seem to think it does."

He turned away, muttering curses and complaints and she stared after him, more angry than she'd been in ages. She was not one to dwell upon resentments, but she was feeling some now. After all she'd done for her family, after all her sacrifices and delayed dreams, she didn't need payment—but she certainly could use a little acceptance and compassion. After all, she was very likely falling in love with a man she would never be able to have for her own. And all because she was trying to save the restaurant. A little family support would be helpful.

"You didn't tell me," he said, turning back. "Why didn't you tell me?"

"Because…"

That was a question. Why hadn't she told him? She usually told him everything. Now that she thought about it, she could see that not telling him made it seem as though she were ashamed, and there was nothing to be ashamed about.

"I guess I didn't want to get your hopes up about the basil," she said, knowing that was lame.

"Oh, Isabella, my beautiful daughter."

His voice echoed with despair. He swayed as though he was about to fall and she hurried to help him stay upright, then gave him an arm as she led him back into the restaurant and through the kitchen where Susa was grating chocolate, into the little room behind where he could rest.

Once she had him settled, she came out and asked Susa, "What on earth is going on? Why is he so upset?"

She shrugged. "He has a point, you know. Nothing good can come from these liaisons with princes."

Isabella threw out her hands. "Sorry, but I beg to differ. Something good has already come from them."

She pointed to the bag of basil. Then her chin rose defiantly.

"And anyway, I like the man and he likes me. We have fun together. End of story."

Susa shook her head, not giving an inch. "That's what they all say when the relationship begins," she noted gloomily. "It's later when reality sets in like crows on the clothesline."

Isabella stared at the older woman. "You have no faith in me, either one of you." She threw up her hands. "Maybe I should just go. Maybe I should go back to the city and forget all about helping out here."

"Maybe you should," Susa said. "But for now, your father is worried about other things besides the precious feelings of his little girl. Fredo Cavelli has filed a formal complaint with the village board."

Isabella whirled, her anger forgotten. "What?"

That really was bad news. If the board actually accepted his complaint, there would be an investigation. They might

have to hire a lawyer to defend their interests. And where would the money come from for something like that?

"Your father says he can fight this on his own," Susa said, shaking her head, when Isabella brought that up. "I say, God help us all."

Isabella sighed. You solved one problem and another jumped up to take its place. Happened every time. So what was she going to do about this one?

"First," she told Susa, "I'm going to write to Cristiano and Valentino to come home and help with this attack on our livelihood." Another flash of anger roiled through her. Why were her brothers never here to help carry some of this burden? "They should be coming home soon for Papa's birthday anyway."

"Are you planning a party?"

Isabella hesitated, then let herself relax a bit. "Of course. Just a family party, but we need to celebrate. Papa needs the moral support, if nothing else."

"I'll start work on a cake right now," Susa said, looking happier.

Isabella frowned fiercely, gathering strength. "Then I'm going to come in here and start a big vat of sauce for the evening dinner rush."

"Good." Susa nodded approvingly. "That'll show them."

Isabella laughed and gave the older woman an affectionate hug. "You better believe it," she agreed, and went off to do just that.

Despite everything, Isabella went to the castle the next day. She and Max rode out on horseback again. This time they took the picnic lunch she brought and spread it out on a cloth at the hillside. The sun was shining, the day was fresh and clear, and something seemed to be sparkling in the air.

For some reason, she found herself telling him about the unpleasant reception she'd had when she got home the day before. A little of her anger still lingered, and he could tell.

"It's because they love you," he told her. "They think they're protecting you."

"They think they're controlling me, you mean," she shot back.

"That too," he admitted. "But I'm sure they're worried about the restaurant and that colors their emotions." He looked at her sideways. "Have you considered taking out a loan to get you through this rough patch?" he asked.

Her heart skipped a beat. He was ready to offer a loan to her family. She could tell by his tentative tone. That was unbelievably generous of him and it warmed her. But she shook her head quickly.

"My father is already up to his chin in loan repayment bills," she told him. "He can't handle any more."

"Hmm."

He looked thoughtful and she smiled. Yes, she could easily fall head over heels for this man. Sadness still haunted the recesses of his eyes, but it didn't seem to dominate his spirit the way it had before. His smile seemed more genuine. And he laughed more. He was opening up to her more than she would have dreamed possible just a few days before.

And that was good, because Isabella had plans. She had ideas. She had projects swirling in her head. She wanted to tell him, but she knew she had to take it slowly so as not to scare him off.

Max had no plans at all. He was enjoying her and enjoying the day, and that was all he thought about. Little by little he began to realize she had more on her mind, but he didn't flinch. As she tentatively brought up the vineyard

and what a shame it was to let it go to waste he listened. He was enchanted by her and her enthusiasms and he didn't want to tell her that her ideas were crazy.

So by the end of the day, they had a compromise of sorts. He would allow her to bring her friend to take a look at the vineyard and give an estimate of what it would take to bring it back into production. And he would give it a fair consideration. Then she would bring more of her restaurant's wonderful famous sauce for him to have on his pasta for his dinner.

She felt good about it. It was so obvious to her that he was ready. She wouldn't be pushing if she weren't sure of that. If what he really wanted was to be alone, that was his choice. But she could tell he was ready to spread his wings. All he needed was the space and the opportunity to fly.

CHAPTER NINE

THE next few days seemed to race by. Isabella went to the castle nearly every day on one pretext or another, and Max was just as complicit as she was in finding reasons she should be there. They seemed to mesh so well, and their interest in each other was new and still overwhelming. Max told Isabella everything he could think of about his childhood, and she still asked for more. Then he quizzed her about the village, about her brothers, about her father's past, about her childhood and her dreams as a young adult.

"I went to library school for a while," she told him. "I was actually thinking of a career in a big university library. I dreamed about going to live in the city, of being a part of the hustle and bustle, the lights and the excitement."

Her eyes shone as she talked about it and he smiled.

"What happened?"

She sighed. "My father got sick. My brothers were both gone, so I came home to help him."

He nodded. It was just what he'd feared. She was the one whose shoulders were supposed to be big enough to carry all the weight. And here she was, ready to take up his concerns as well.

He asked more about the restaurant and she filled him

in. Once she started, it was as if she'd opened the flood-gates and she opened up about her worries for her father, about the state of the family finances and how worried she was about the haphazard way her father had managed things. And finally, she even told him about the problems with Fredo Cavelli.

Max frowned as he listened to all this. "Can he really do any damage to your restaurant?" he asked.

She thought for a moment. "You know, I didn't think so until very recently. He was always just an old grouch who had a grudge against my father. But now that he's become big friends with the mayor and managed to get a seat on the planning commission, he's starting to make me nervous."

He listened sympathetically, nodding and asking intelligent questions at all the right times. And she realized he was the first person she'd ever told all these things to. Suddenly that seemed very, very significant to her.

"If it's money your father needs," he began.

"No," she said quickly. "You are generous to a fault, Max. But my father needs more than money right now. He needs his family to get together and help him."

Max nodded. "Now, that's up to you to handle," he told her. "You're the one they will all listen to."

"What?" She couldn't imagine where he could have got that idea. "No one listens to me."

He gave her a penetrating look. "They will if you let them know how important the family is to you, and to them. Try it. I think you'll be surprised." He squeezed her hand. "And in the meantime, if your father has more trouble with the board, I might be able to make a few phone calls and pull a few strings myself."

She loved that he was offering, but couldn't foresee a time when his help could really make a difference. He still

didn't leave the castle walls. But his other advice was sound and she took it to heart.

She marveled at how her life had changed in such a short time. Who would have believed that she would so quickly become so at home in the castle? And so very happy there. The place seemed to be timeless, ageless, forever. If only that could really be true.

To her surprise, Renzo had become an ally of sorts. She'd been straightforward with him from the beginning.

"You know what I'm trying to do, don't you?" she asked him one day while Max was on the telephone with a researcher he often collaborated with.

"No, miss." The man looked more like a walking skeleton every day. "Perhaps you should explain it to me."

Isabella took a deep breath and searched for the right words. "I guess I would say that I'm trying to find a way to get the prince to come out of his shell a little, to take part in the wider life of the community he lives in."

"Ah."

She couldn't read a thing in that reaction.

"He's been living here, away from everyone else, though wonderfully protected by you and his family, for almost ten years now."

"Yes, miss."

"Do you think it's been good for him?"

Renzo hesitated. "Well, I do think that a large part of him has healed over that time."

She smiled, relieved. She'd been so afraid he would take offense at what she was doing. "Oh, I'm so glad to hear you say that. So you agree with me that it is time for him to branch out a bit?"

She held her breath, waiting to see what his verdict was.

"Yes. Yes, I do."

She closed her eyes and laughed a little. "Thank goodness. I was afraid…"

"No, miss," he said stoutly. "I will help you in any way I can."

She took his hand and shook it vigorously. "Thank you, Mr. Renzo. Thank you so much."

"I've known him since he was a boy," Renzo continued solemnly. "He's a wonderful man, you know. He's suffered too much. He deserves more out of life than what he's been given so far."

"We agree on that."

He nodded. He didn't quite smile, but she had a feeling he never did. "I could see from the first that you were a good-hearted lady," he went on. "I just want to help."

It was such a relief not to have to fight against Max's oldest employee and closest companion. Just knowing that he was in her corner gave her courage and she didn't waste any time.

The very next day, she brought in her friend the contractor to take a look at the vineyards. Having been warned ahead about what to expect and how she wanted him to act around Max, Giancarlo did fine. His face did register a bit of shock when he first caught sight of the scars, but he quickly settled down and treated Max like anyone at all.

So far so good. Now to convince him that the large mentioned sum would be worth the effort in expenditure. Giancarlo put up a pretty good argument and Max promised to think it over. The contractor left and Max didn't seem unduly bothered by the entire process. She breathed another sigh of relief.

And when Giancarlo returned the next day with a wine expert, just to give Max more information, that meeting went just fine as far as she could see.

To her eyes, he seemed to be blossoming. Little by little, he was beginning to be able to accept others in a way he hadn't been able to do for so long. She told him as much that day as they sat out on the veranda and ate a simple lunch.

"I think you've developed a sort of paranoia by living alone for so long," she told him. "Most people are perfectly willing to accept people who are different, once they get used to it. It's the surprise that gets them at first. Then, when they realize it's only skin-deep, they are usually okay with it."

"You've made a detailed study of this, I presume?" he teased her.

"Sure," she shot back. "Live and let live is the motto of our age," she added with a flourish meant to overwhelm his doubts.

He shook his head and his mouth twisted with his signature cynicism. "You're dreaming."

She gave him a mock glare. "If so, it's a good dream. Why not join me?"

He shrugged. He knew what she meant. She was so set on his starting off on this project. "Tell me this, Bella, why does the world need a Rossi vineyard?"

She leaned forward, her eyes big. "It's not just that. You need to be a part of your community. And just think of the jobs you could provide. People around here could live better lives, all because of you."

He bit back a grin. "What if I don't care if all those anonymous people I've never met are getting jobs or not?"

"You should care," she maintained stoutly. "That's why you have to go out and meet them. Then you'll care."

He groaned, but he didn't tell her to stop planning.

She brought in plants to fill in a bare spot in the gardens at the mausoleum. She loved going there, loved looking at the statue that reminded her of Max. He went along with her

and helped break up the soil. And he told her about his beautiful mother and how she'd loved this garden. And somehow he went on to describe how destroyed she'd been when the people had turned against her as her looks had faded.

"For some reason, when a woman is that beautiful, it becomes the most important thing about her," Isabella said, agreeing with him. "Nothing else she does, no matter how much genius it displays, is held to the same esteem."

He nodded, thinking of his mother. "The celebrity culture needs its routine sacrifices, and she was one of them."

Isabella put a hand on his knee and looked up into his huge dark eyes. She knew very well that what had happened to his mother had colored how he looked at his own loss of beauty.

"It's very sad, but you can't let it affect you."

He smiled down at her, but he knew she was right. It had affected him. And it was high time he reversed that process.

Later that evening, Isabella got up the nerve to ask Renzo a very sensitive question. She'd made dinner for the three of them and was in the kitchen, gathering her supplies and getting ready to head home. Max was off doing some research on the Internet.

"Tell me something, Renzo," she said, turning to find him preparing breadcrumbs from the leftover garlic bread for toasting. "I know the prince was scarred in an accident, but I don't know much about the details. Are you willing to tell me what happened?"

She watched his eyes to see how he would react to that question but he didn't give away any clues.

"Have you asked him?"

She shook her head. "He's never volunteered the information and I don't want to make him relive it if it's just too painful for him. But if you'd rather not say…"

Slowly, he shook his head. "I think it would be better if you talked to him about it directly, miss."

Sighing, she nodded. She knew he was right. Walking out onto the terrace, she looked up at the stars. She remembered the day he'd told her about how Laura had died. Could she really ask him to do this as well? It seemed she was going to have to.

Max came out to join her a short time later.

"Max, I need to know. About your scars…" She raised her hand and touched his face. "How did it happen?"

His hand covered hers. "Do you want the official story? Or the truth?"

She searched his eyes. His words were bitter but his gaze was clear. "Don't they say the truth will set you free?" she asked softly.

"They say a lot of things meant to sound smart that are nothing but hot-air balloons," he told her, thrusting his hands deep into his pockets. "Okay, Bella, you asked for it. Here goes." He tilted his head back as though searching for the Milky Way. "It happened the night Laura died."

Her heart lurched. She'd been afraid of that.

"I raced her lifeless body to the hospital, knowing there was really no hope, but praying some miracle might happen. They tried. They did everything humanly possible. But she…" His voice choked and he paused for a moment, regaining his composure.

She put her hand over her heart, aching with the pain he must have felt that day. She rocked back and forth, wishing she could take it from him somehow. But that could never happen. It was his burden to hold forever. All she could do was hope, in some simple way, to help him deal with it.

"She was still dead," he said as he went on, his voice

rough. "They couldn't perform miracles and I found I had no magic powers either. It was hopeless. I was hopeless. I had just let my wife and my unborn child die while I lay snoozing a few feet away."

He turned to look at her, his eyes burning. "The horror of that, the pain and the guilt, were just too deep to bear. As I drove myself home, I found myself going faster and faster. I couldn't think of a reason to slow down. I no longer had anything to live for. The rest of my life would be hell on earth. What was the point?"

"Oh, Max. You didn't…"

He winced. "I aimed straight for that tree. All I could think of was joining Laura." He looked at her again. "So now you know."

"Yes." She barely whispered the word. In trying to end his suffering, he'd only made his own suffering worse—but perhaps that was what he'd wanted to do. She nodded. It didn't really surprise her. But she felt such utter sadness. He'd made his own hellish prison on earth and now he didn't know how to break out of it. She didn't speak. Her throat was choked with unshed tears. But she understood better now. She knew he'd created his own special torture. He'd locked himself away here because he thought he deserved it. It wasn't just that he didn't like the way people reacted to his face—he thought of it as a punishment. He thought he deserved never to connect with the rest of humanity. It was his lot in life, his life sentence, and he had no right to try to overturn it.

No reprieves for the Rossi prince.

Finally, tears filled her eyes and she could cry. She tried to turn away, but he wouldn't let her. Gently, carefully, he took her into his arms and held her close. And she cried.

She cried for Laura, and the tiny baby. She cried for Max and his mountain of pain. And she cried for herself.

"Don't cry, Bella," he said at last. "I only got what I deserved."

And that only made her start sobbing all over again.

Finally, she pulled back and looked up into his face, half laughing, wiping away the tears.

"Look, I've ruined your shirt," she said, putting her hand over the wet spots and feeling his heart beating very hard beneath her palm, as though he'd been running, as though he were feeling…

Her own heart began to pump in response. And then she looked up at him, her lips parted, waiting.

He looked down and she could see the struggle behind his eyes. He wanted to kiss her as much as she wanted it herself. Why, oh, why was he fighting it?

It was a question that was bothering her more and more lately. She'd never felt anything this close to love before, not with any man. She wanted to tell him so. She wanted his arms around her; she wanted his mouth on hers. She wanted his kiss.

He'd kissed her the day she'd let herself into his house with her sauce for him to sample. The entire encounter had been unexpected and he hadn't been prepared. His defenses had been down. His kiss had been spiced with a wildness that he'd quickly leashed, but she had been able to sense it flowing just under the surface. He'd been so gorgeous with his naked chest and his wet hair. Her heart beat like thunder whenever she thought of it.

She knew he cared for her. She even knew that he felt a strong attraction. A connection of excitement arced between them every time their gazes met across a room. When he helped put on her cloak in the evening, his fingers

lingered on the slope of her neck and she knew he was aching to let his hands slide down and cup her breasts. She could feel it. And still he didn't kiss her.

She turned quickly once, wearing a light and skimpy vest-top, and let her breasts brush against the hair on his bare arm, making her nipples harden beneath the cloth. He watched her do it and the chords of his neck stood out like a mountain range while the color of his eyes deepened almost to purple. He clenched his fists and she knew it was taking a tremendous effort for him not to reach for her.

But he didn't. The moment passed, and he turned away as though he couldn't bear to look at her any longer.

She knew what the problem was. He didn't foresee any possibility that their light and friendly relationship would last, or that it could turn into anything meaningful, and he didn't want to set up any expectations in her mind. She knew he was probably right, but when she was with him, she hardly cared. She just wanted to touch him, to kiss him, to glory in the feeling they had between them.

So she waited, her lips parted, her eyes dreamy, and practically begged him to bend down and take control.

"Isabella," he began, his voice slightly choked. *"Cara mia."* He was shaking his head.

"Max!" She grabbed his arm and glared up at him. "If you don't kiss me, I'm going to walk out that door and never come back!"

His dark eyes warmed and then he was laughing at her again. "Bella," he said affectionately, reaching up to rake his fingers through the hair behind her shell-like ear. "You're lying."

"You think I won't do it?" she demanded wildly.

He pulled her closer. "I know you won't," he said, his warm breath singeing her lips. "But this should seal the deal."

And he kissed her.

All her wildness dissolved at his touch. This was what she'd been waiting for—living for. His mouth on hers was hot and his tongue was rough and his arms were hard with masculine strength that took her breath away. She could feel his hunger and it sent a sense of relief through her. He wanted her as much as she wanted him.

She could let go. She could sink into this feeling without fear, and she did, opening up her soul as she opened her heart. Her fingers sank into his thick hair, pulling him up harder against where she was arched, trying to feel as much of him as she could.

With her mouth, her tongue, her hands, her body, she was telling him, *Here I am. Take me. I'm yours.*

His hard, beautiful hands slid down her sides to her back and then cupped her bottom, pressing her even closer into the refuge of his hips. He knew it would take only seconds to lose himself in the heat of her kiss and let it build into something more serious. The urgency he'd been keeping under such tight control was stirring and he knew just how dangerous that could be. He should pull back and let her understand what she was risking.

But he couldn't do it—not yet. He'd had dreams about how it could be with them, and to have her in his arms like this made it all seem so much more possible. As he explored her mouth, her skin, her ear, she seemed to melt at his touch, as though she were made to love him.

"Bella," he moaned, his mind foggy with desire. *"Cara mia."*

She murmured something but he didn't know what she was saying. He was lost in the vortex. In another moment, he would be over the edge. He had to turn this back. He pulled his head away, groaning from a place deep inside.

His vision was blurred, but she looked like a goddess, too tempting to resist. Still, he managed.

"Bella, no," he muttered against her ear. "We have to stop."

She sighed, but she didn't argue. She pulled back away from him so that nothing was touching, but then she leaned her face close again and kissed him. Lips to lips, heart to heart. How could he turn that away? They'd gone from sweetness to searing fire and back to sweetness again.

The kiss went on and on. If she had her way, it would never stop.

She knew it now—she knew he was hers, at least for the moment, and she was flooded with a feeling of lightness and joy, as though a thousand angels were singing a Beethoven chorus in her heart.

This was good. This was the way things ought to be.

But the beautiful singing ended abruptly, like a scratch on a record, when Max's sister Angela entered the room.

"Well, excuse me," she said, but she didn't go back out again. Instead, she stood where she was and waited for them to compose themselves.

"Angela," Max said, turning reluctantly and straightening his shirt and not looking the least bit uncomfortable. "To what do we owe this unexpected visit?"

"I don't know how it can be unexpected when I told you I was coming back here this weekend."

"Oh." He frowned. "That's right. There's been so much going on around here, I'd forgotten all about that."

"So it seems." She pretended to smile. "So nice to see you again, Isabella. I hope the restaurant is doing well?"

"Yes, thank you," Isabella answered, trying to play this as cool as Max was, but knowing she wasn't quite as unruffled as he. She'd finally got Max to throw away his inhibitions and really kiss him, and now this!

"Very good." Angela gave her brother a scathing glance. "Well, I'll just go unpack my things. It seems Renzo forgot I was coming as well." She started out the door, then looked back and said with a touch of amused irony, "I'm beginning to feel downright unwelcome." And just before she disappeared, she made a face that almost made Isabella like her.

"You'd better go," Max told her. He touched her cheek and looked as if he might kiss her again, but then he didn't. "See you tomorrow?" he asked, regret in his eyes.

"Of course," she responded.

But she was the one who harbored the most remorse. Something told her this kiss hadn't really started a trend, and it was going to be just as much of an effort on her part before she got him to do it again. If only he could believe in something good between the two of them. If only she could convince him it might work.

But even thinking that surprised her, because it meant she'd begun to hope—maybe a little too much? Time would tell.

Angela stayed for three days but Isabella only spent time alone with her once. She was polite enough, but she seemed very skeptical about Isabella's place in the scheme of things.

"I understand you're lobbying for some big changes around here," she said as they came face-to-face in the kitchen one morning.

Isabella lifted her chin. "Yes, in fact, I am."

Angela raised one sleek eyebrow. "We all know Max has been lonely for a long time. It wouldn't be difficult for a pretty young woman like you to cast a spell that led him into something he wasn't prepared for. Something totally inappropriate."

Isabella took a deep breath. Angela seemed to think she

could be cowed. How interesting. Angela was going to have to think again.

"I think you underestimate your brother. Of course he's as capable of a flirtation as any man, but he's as careful and cynical as any man I've ever known as well. He's certainly nobody's pushover."

Angela's eyes widened. "Of course not. I didn't mean to imply any such thing." She frowned. "But, Isabella, it's plain as the nose on your face. You two are crazy about each other right now. The air fairly sizzles between you." She hesitated and looked suspicious. "You're not...?"

"No. No, we're not."

She nodded, looking relieved. "Well, I'm sure you understand that his family will have a say in any major decisions he makes about his future."

Isabella blinked. Did she mean what it sounded like she meant? "Angela, if you're worried we're going to run off and elope or something, I think you can rest easy on that score. I have no plans to try to snare your brother."

Angela nodded skeptically. "Plans are one thing, the heat of passion is another."

Isabella was trying hard to hold her temper.

"I don't think you should worry. I understand that he has duties and responsibilities to a larger universe than the relationship he and I have together. A different universe than the one I come from. I don't have any fantasies on that score."

Angela nodded. "Well, I'm pleased to see you have a head on your shoulders."

Isabella smiled. "On the other hand, if Max decides to do something, I don't think you will have a hope in heaven of stopping him."

Angela winced, then gave Isabella a penetrating look. "Tell me this. Do you think you are in love with my brother?"

She drew her breath in sharply. She could be blunt, but that would be offensive. So she rounded the edges a little. "Honestly, that is not something I've been thinking about. Much, anyway," she added softly.

Angela's eyes flashed. "So you won't tell me one way or another."

Isabella finally let her anger spill out. "Angela, I don't actually think it's any of your business how I feel about Max. I owe you a certain regard and a certain common courtesy, but I'm not going to spill out the inner workings of my heart and brain for you to pore over. Those are mine alone."

Angela stared at her for a long moment, then, unexpectedly, she laughed.

"Good answer," she said. "And I like you the better for it."

And that was the end of that encounter.

They all breathed a sigh of relief when Angela decamped. It allowed them to go back to the comfortable atmosphere they'd had before she came and it gave Isabella a bit of room to try to convince Max he should renovate the vineyards.

"Just look at the majesty of all this," she said as they walked through a portion where the grape plants still had green shoots and looked recoverable. "Can you imagine what it would be like?"

"There's something to that," Max mused as they strolled along. "There is something rejuvenating about plants that lose their leaves and then come back like the phoenix to show off their glory again."

"The rebirth of hope," she agreed.

"Yes." He nodded, his head to the side thoughtfully, and she smiled. She was winning. She could feel it.

"Watch out." His arm shot out to protect her from a broken stake, and then he was curling her into his arms. "Isabella," he said warningly.

She laughed, pressing against him with sheer joy in the body contact. "I didn't do this," she protested. "It was all you."

He kissed her softly and let her go and she sighed, wanting more, knowing she was going to have to wait. "Let's sit here by this little rose garden," she said, shielding her eyes from the sun. "It's hot out here today."

They sat in the shade and looked out over the plants again. "Have you thought about the estimate Giancarlo gave you?" she asked.

He nodded. "I could buy a new yacht for what he wants," he said. "A racing yacht and a racing crew to go with it."

"Oh." She was disappointed. "Is it really too much?"

"Yes," he said. "Tell me this, Bella. If you had a lot of money, what would you use it for?"

She thought for a moment. He probably expected her to say she would throw it away on his vineyards. Or help the poor. Or some other noble gesture. But she had another project in mind.

She looked at him and wondered if she dared say it. Taking a deep breath, she prepared for the worst.

"Max, if I had enough money, I would hire the best surgeon in the world to do something about the scars on your face."

He stared at her, shocked. "What?"

She reached out for his hand. "Not because I want you to change," she told him quickly. "I've told you before that I think you are the most beautiful man in the world, and your scars only make you more precious to me. But I would like to see you lose them because I want you to stop punishing yourself. Ten years is long enough. You deserve a pardon."

Picking up her hand, he brought it to his lips and opened it so that he could kiss her palm. "I don't need a pardon," he said softly, looking up at her through her spread fingers. "*Bella mia*, I have you."

Her heart seemed to swell at his words. Were they only meant in play? She couldn't be sure.

"Tell me, Max. Have you ever looked into surgery?"

He shook his head. "No."

"I knew it. You haven't even tried."

"You're right."

"I've seen some amazing things done with—"

"No." He dropped her hand and looked almost stern. "I could never do that."

She searched his eyes. "Why not?"

He shrugged and looked away. "You said it yourself. This is my punishment."

His voice hardened as he turned back to look deep into her eyes.

"Bella, I slept while my wife and child died in front of me. Don't you think I deserve a little pain for that?"

"No." She was passionate about that. "No, not at all. You've had enough pain to last a lifetime."

Their gazes held for a long moment. Finally, Max tried to smile. "So you see, we disagree." His smile widened as he studied her pretty face and took up her hand again.

"Bella, Bella, you take these things too hard." He kissed her fingers, one by one. "Maybe I should get a mask like that fellow in *Phantom of the Opera*. Do you think that would suit me?"

She'd settled down by now and could joke with him if that was what he wanted.

"I don't know." She pretended to consider it, then looked at him sharply. "How well do you sing?"

He looked surprised. "Oh, you have to sing?"

"Sure. It goes with the territory."

They laughed together. It was good to laugh. Laughter

took some of the sting out of the pain. And Lord knew she was ready to do anything she could to do that for him.

"Okay, Bella," he said finally, dropping her hand again. "Call your friend Giancarlo. We'll see if we can work something out on renovating a portion of the field."

"Oh!" She threw her arms around his neck and kissed his cheek. "Oh, I'm so glad!" She stopped. "But wait, only a portion?"

He nodded. "For now, greedy little lady. We'll just take this one step at a time."

"Oh. Of course." She calmed herself down. Naturally he wanted to see how having a few workmen around worked out for him before he committed to a huge operation. It was only logical. She was just happy he'd decided to take this step at all.

"Okay." She sighed happily. "We'll do it your way."

He gave her an adorably crooked grin. "What other way is there?"

CHAPTER TEN

AFTER spending so much time with Max, Isabella finally had to admit that she needed to concentrate on just how much her own family was making her crazy. Everything should be going swimmingly. They had the herb again. People were flocking to the restaurant just as they had in the best days of the past. You would think everyone would be happy with that—but no. There was a constant drumbeat of concern for her relationship with the prince, from her family and from everyone else, too.

Everyone in town seemed to know about it now, and each and every one had to stick his nose into it and give her the benefit of his or her great advice.

"Isabella, don't you think it is time to get over this obsession with the Rossi prince? He's not for you. You know how these things turn out, every time. You may be happy with it now, but in the end he'll want another sort of woman, a woman he can marry, and you'll be stuck with the consequences of your time with him."

That trend of thought was the most annoying, because it was very difficult to answer. She could either get mad, or walk away. She usually did the latter.

Her father was the most troubling because she knew he really did care about her and was genuinely worried.

"Where are you going?" he seemed to ask every time she came near a door. "When will you be back? You're not going to go see *him* again, are you?"

She was very careful not to take too much time away from the restaurant. She knew he needed her help and she didn't resent that at all. In fact, she wanted to make him feel less anxious, if only she knew how. Talking didn't seem to do it. And she decided a lot of it was based on his worry about the threats from Fredo—and those were beginning to worry her, too.

"Papa, what does he have against you?" she asked him again and again. "Why is he doing this?"

"He worked with me when I first had my stand on the Via Roma. We argued. He went off to start his own place, which failed. For years he's claimed I stole his recipes. Even after he opened his ice cream store, he told everyone my success was due to his recipes."

"Does he have even a tiny, tiny justification for thinking that?"

"Not a bit. He never even knew where I got the basil. He's just a crazy, angry old fool."

But crazy, angry old fools could do a lot of damage.

She went to a planning committee meeting with her father. He was too weak to stand up and speak his mind, so she did it for him and the arguing got pretty heated for a while. Even after all that, she wasn't totally clear on what the issue was and she didn't have a good feeling about things.

"What is it that you want?" she demanded of Fredo at one point. "Do you want us to admit guilt? Do you want money? What?"

Fredo was sitting in his chair at the long table and giving her his evil look. "I want Luca to lose his business like I lost mine." That was all he would say.

"The problem is," her father said as they were walking home from the meeting, "now that he has the mayor's ear and a seat on the planning commission, he thinks he can put the screws to me." He shook his head. "At first I was wondering if your aunt Lisa might not be behind it all. But he's gone further than even she would now."

"Oh, Papa. Aunt Lisa loves you deep down."

"Hah!" He shook his head. "A lot you know about it."

Luca's sister Lisa was a very different type from plain, sweet Luca. Isabella knew her well, though she had a way of flitting in and out of life in Monta Correnti, despite having a very successful restaurant right next to the one her brother ran. Lisa also had a habit of bestowing different fathers on each of her three daughters, all cousins to Isabella. Scarlett, who was just her age, had been a close friend when they were young. But the two of them had been involved in some childish antics that had put a pall on their friendship and to this day their secret was like a barrier between them and they seldom spoke.

But her aunt Lisa did enough talking to make up for it.

"Well, I hear you're flying high these days," she said, meeting Isabella in the courtyard outside their respective restaurants.

Isabella decided to play dumb. "What are you talking about?"

"Running with royalty, they say."

She bit her tongue. She couldn't explain to Lisa how it had all come about, because that would be giving away the secret of the basil, something only a few people knew about. When you came right down to it, Lisa was the last person they would want to know. In many ways, she and Luca were in direct competition and had been for years. If Lisa found out about the basil, Isabella knew she would get

her hands on it immediately and hire the best chefs from Rome to come try out new recipes. As if they didn't have enough trouble with declining revenue at Rosa as it was. If Lisa took over the basil and began to promote it as only she knew how, they would be sunk.

"I've always heard he's such a recluse he won't even allow tradesmen at the palazzo. But suddenly he's hobnobbing with our little Izzy." Lisa gave her a flippant look. "If I'd known he was so easy to get to, I'd have been out there to see him myself."

A flare of panic rose in Isabella's throat. What if she tried it? "What would you want to see him about?" she asked, frowning.

"I'd invite him to dinner, of course." Lisa smiled. She knew she'd hit a nerve. "Can you imagine the promotional possibilities? I'm surprised you haven't had him in to your place yet. But I suppose that's to come. Isn't it?"

She shook her head. She really had to head off this thinking at the pass if she could.

"It's not like that, Aunt Lisa. I've been doing some consulting with him. He has some projects he's thinking of tackling and I'm putting him in touch with local experts."

"Is he thinking of starting a restaurant? I can't imagine you know much about anything else."

That did it. Lack of respect from relatives was a deal breaker as far as she was concerned. If her aunt couldn't even pretend to have some deference for her, she was toast.

"You'd be surprised what I know about, Aunt Lisa," she said icily, turning away. "You might want to think about that before you get involved in things you don't understand." She looked back at Lisa. To her surprise, the woman was looking flustered. "I would hate to think certain rumors might come back to bite you where my cousins are concerned."

Lisa looked downright startled and Isabella had a twinge of guilt. She didn't actually have a lot of juicy rumors about her aunt, but she was pretty sure there were some out there. So let her stew!

"She's just so arrogant," she explained to Max later that day as they were riding out across the estate, heading for another feast of tapas at the Spanish stand outside the walls. "I can't abide that."

"Forget about her," he advised. "We have a long, lazy afternoon with no one else but each other. Let's enjoy it."

That sounded good to her. He was in a good mood because work had started on the vineyards and he'd actually gone down and done a bit of supervising. No one had blanched at his scars. No one had turned green and gone behind a tree to vomit, something that had actually happened to him once at a seaside resort. He was feeling pretty good about prospects for the future. Maybe he could have something of a normal life after all.

They tied the horses and he went to sit at a table overlooking the river, while Isabella headed for the stand to get the food. She went inside and greeted Señor Ortega. He began talking the moment she entered and she laughed because it was obvious he was going to go on talking even after she was out of sight. She picked out some spiced clams, some corn fritters, some fried black pudding, some stuffed mushrooms, and nice cold beer for Max. Señor Ortega fried up some special samosas for her, and as he did the most beautiful little girl came into the store. Tiny and small-boned, she had a halo of light curls that flew around her pretty face like a cloud of spun gold.

"This is Ninita," Señor Ortega told her proudly. "My first grandchild."

"I'm pleased to meet you, Ninita," Isabella said, shaking

the child's hand and getting a solemn smile in return. "What a beautiful child," she said sotto voce to the man behind the bar.

"Yes, she is my angel," he said. "Here, take this tray. You've ordered so much food, I'll help you carry it out."

"Can I help too?" Ninita asked sweetly.

"Of course, my darling," said the older man. "Here, you can carry the napkins."

They formed a small train, carrying everything to the table where Max sat waiting.

"We come bearing lots of delicious tapas," Isabella said as they approached. "And we have help from Señor Ortega's grandchild. Meet little Ninita. Ninita, this is Prince Max."

The little girl had been carefully carrying the napkins and now she looked up, eager to meet a real live prince. Her face registered her shock as she saw him. Isabella saw what was happening as if in slow motion. She knew she had to stop it. She tried. But it was too late. The little girl took in a loud, gasping breath, dropped the napkins and threw her hands over her face. Then she began to scream as though she'd seen something horrible. Turning, she ran as fast as her little legs would carry her, screaming all the way.

Max sat very still. His face was drained of all color. Señor Ortega was apologizing profusely, and Max tried to smile as he waved away the older man's regrets. But the gaze that met Isabella's horrified eyes was full of self-loathing. As soon as Señor Ortega went back into the shop Max rose from where he was sitting. Without saying a word, he strode toward his horse and mounted, and before Isabella could say anything at all he was gone, too.

She stood there, holding the tray, knowing something very terrible had just happened—knowing it was going to

change things. Something deep inside her was clenched like a fist and she was afraid it was going to be a long time before that feeling went away.

It was over an hour later before Isabella found Max, sitting by the river in a part of the estate she'd never seen before. She slid off Mimi's back and went to sit beside him. But when she reached out to take his hand, he pulled it away, then looked at her with eyes as cold as ice.

"It's over, Isabella. Our idyllic interlude is done."

She stared at him, aghast. "What are you talking about?"

"I thought I could elude my fate, but of course I was wrong. My crime is advertised on my face. I can't escape. I may fool myself for a while, but in the end it comes back to haunt me."

"Max, don't talk like that. It was my fault. I should have prepared her…"

He swore. "Can you prepare the whole world, Bella? I think not."

"But, Max…"

"Isabella, can't you see?" He turned his dark, tragic eyes on her. "I can't do this. I can't go out and mix with the world if I'm going to make precious little girls scream. I don't have the right to do that to them."

Suddenly it was clear to her that she had misunderstood his entire mental state. She'd thought he was shrinking from the pain of seeing how people reacted to his face. But he was way beyond that by now. It was evident to her that his motivations were very different. He was trying to avoid giving pain to others by inflicting his very disturbing scars on them.

And what could she possibly do about that? She couldn't control what others thought when they saw him. She stared into the water and felt a wave of hopelessness that wasn't

like her. She was done. She had no more ideas, no more plans and projects. She had tried. And now it was over.

Turning so he wouldn't see the tears in her eyes, she rose and went to where Mimi was tied. In a moment, she was over the ridge and out of his sight. And then she let the tears fall like rain.

She spent the next week working hard at the restaurant, trying to develop some ideas for her father, ideas that would help brighten up the place. She hadn't been able to generate much interest as yet, but she was determined to try harder. Something would come of it yet.

She hadn't heard anything at all from Max, but she hadn't been able to think of much else. She missed him. She needed him. She was so in love…why hadn't she realized that before? She'd been in denial. Now that she'd lost him, she knew it was true. She loved him with all her heart. But what could she do about it?

She heard he'd paid off the workmen and sent everyone home. There were to be no more Rossi vineyards. She also heard a group from town had gone out to talk to him about using the estate for a fundraiser for the Monta Correnti Beautification Committee. He had refused to see them. He was doing just what he'd said he would do—reverting to his normal life. And that had no room for her in it.

Could it really be all over so soon? It seemed so. It truly hurt to have finally found a man whom she knew she could love with all her heart and soul, a man whose mind and interests fit nicely into the scope of her own, a man whose touch sent thrills through her body and created an ache of longing where her feminine secrets lay—and then have to give him up this way. But her life, as usual, was a less than stellar existence.

Okay, now she was whining and feeling very sorry for herself. But didn't she deserve to? Yes—though she knew very well too much of that self-indulgence could ruin a good summer if she didn't watch out. She gave herself one more day to mope about and cry, and then she was going to move on and find a place for herself where she could count for something and make a difference.

There. Just making a plan made her feel so much better.

Unfortunately, life had made its own plans and they didn't take hers into account. She was sitting in the kitchen, shelling peas with Susa, when a young man arrived to serve Luca with a writ of failure to comply with a permit ordinance. The warrant stated that he had been deemed to be in noncompliance and, unless he paid an exorbitant fine, he would have to vacate the restaurant premises within forty-eight hours.

Isabella was numb as she read it over to her father again and he struggled to understand what it meant.

"It means we lose the restaurant," she told him, unable to think straight, unable to understand much of this herself. "There is a meeting of the licensing board in two days. Unless we pay the fine by then, we have to pack up and get out."

"No," Luca said, banging his cane into the floor. "Not one cent for those bastards!"

"But, Papa…"

"I'll never give in to Fredo's blackmail. Never."

There wasn't much point in arguing with him. They didn't have the money to pay the fine anyway. She sighed and made plans to attend the meeting. All she could think of was to plead their case with the mayor. Surely he wouldn't be so hard-hearted as to kick them out of their own restaurant, the only means of survival for their family!

But a little place in her head told her there wasn't going to be much hope.

"Once your luck starts to go downhill," Susa intoned gloomily, "it just doesn't stop until it hits bottom."

Could Susa be right? Isabella shuddered and turned her head away.

Max sat out on the veranda, staring into the sunset, his eyes clouded, brooding. He'd thought it would be effortless to slip back into his old life, but in actuality it wasn't. In fact, it was hell on earth. He'd had a certain peace before, but now that was ruined. It sort of reminded him of that old World War I song, "How You Gonna Keep Them Down on the Farm, After They've Seen Paree?" He'd found out, once again, what it was to have a warm and wonderful woman in his life, and without her he felt as if a limb had been removed. Twenty times a day he started to call her. Twenty times a day he caught himself in time.

This was very different from losing Laura. That had been so full of agonizing pain and deep, deep guilt, he'd felt as though he'd been torn apart by red-hot pokers nightly—and that had gone on for years. This pain had very little guilt attached to it. Lots of regret, but not much guilt. Laura had been the love of his youth. Isabella was the joy of his maturity.

Strangely enough, he hadn't felt very guilty about putting memories of Laura to one side while he went about the sweet torture of falling for Isabella. In a funny way, he'd actually thought Laura might approve.

But that was all over now. He felt like a man re-condemned to a life sentence in a cold, lonely prison after he'd had a taste of freedom. It wasn't pleasant.

He looked at the bottle he'd brought out with him. He'd thought he would spend an evening drinking away his sorrows. But somehow he'd lost his thirst. He knew very

well the bottom of a bottle was its own special hell. He didn't need another one.

Renzo came out to see if he needed anything, then lingered a moment, and Max could tell he wanted to say something.

"What is it, Renzo? Spit it out, man."

Renzo coughed. "Sir, I thought I'd mention, I went into the village this afternoon to see Miss Isabella."

"What?" He turned to stare at the man. "What did you do that for?"

"She had left some cooking equipment that I thought she might be missing, so I drove over to drop it by the restaurant."

"Oh." He looked away. He shouldn't ask. He knew the rules. A clean break was the best way. No, he wouldn't ask. He drew his breath in deeply, and then the words came out as though on their own.

"How…how did she seem? Is she all right?"

"I don't know."

He sat up straighter. "What do you mean, you don't know?"

"She wasn't there. I talked to an old woman named Susa who works for Isabella and her father. She said the two of them were over at the town meeting room preparing for an important meeting where they will have to fight to keep those crooks who run the city council from taking their restaurant away."

"Oh, no." Max swore and shook his head. "On what grounds?"

"Something about forgetting to file a permit and the fine being too high to pay."

He nodded. "A put-up job," he said bitterly.

"I'm afraid so, sir."

"Poor Isabella." A slight smile curled his lip. "Good thing she's got spunk. I bet she'll be able to save things on her own."

"You think so, sir?" Renzo said doubtfully.

"Sure. She's amazing." He glanced at Renzo, then away again. "It will be interesting to see how she does it. Keep me informed any time you find out anything new. I want to know how this comes out."

"Very well, sir." Renzo bowed out, looking puzzled.

Max sighed. He knew Renzo wanted him to ride in to the rescue. Didn't he understand how impossible that was? If he didn't get it yet, he would soon. Because Max couldn't have done anything even if he'd wanted to.

Closing his eyes, he saw Isabella's perfect face, and he groaned. The image seemed so real. She was saying something, trying to get him to do something, urging him to get up off his chair and...

He couldn't quite catch what it was, but the image stayed with him into the night, and the dreams he had were even clearer. Isabella needed help. He woke up and stared at the ceiling. Did he have the nerve to do what it would take to help her? That was the part that bothered him. He wasn't sure he did.

It was late in the afternoon of the next day that he received a visitor he wasn't expecting. Of course, since he didn't receive visitors at all, anyone would have been a surprise. But this one was special.

Renzo interrupted him just as he was finishing up some Internet research.

"There's someone here who would like a word with you," he said.

"What are you talking about?" he demanded, wondering if the man had lost his mind.

Renzo hesitated. "Sir, I know this man. He is a very good man. He runs a small tapas stand—"

"Señor Ortega?"

"Yes. You know him, then?"

"Of course." Max frowned. What on earth could the man want? He thought for a moment. Really, it seemed silly to deny him a short visit. "Send him in," he told Renzo. "I'll be happy to see him."

Renzo looked a bit startled, but readily complied, and in another moment Señor Ortega was in the library and shaking Max's hand effusively.

"Thank you so much, your honor," he said, bowing at the same time. "I have a small favor to ask of you. If you would be so kind."

"Por supuesto," Max said, speaking in the man's own language. "What can I do for you?"

"Do you remember the little girl who was there the last time you and Isabella came to eat at my stand?"

Max stiffened. How could he forget? "Yes," he said, his jaw tightening. "What about her?"

"Do you remember that she had a bad reaction to your…" He made a gesture to indicate the scarring on Max's face.

Max stared at Señor Ortega. The man was talking easily about his scars, as though they were just a part of life, not something to be whispered about and avoided at all costs.

"Yes," he said slowly. "I remember."

"Well, she feels so badly about how she acted. She's so ashamed. She asks me every day if we will see you again. She wants to apologize."

Max found himself smiling. "She has nothing to apologize for," he noted dryly. "I'm the one who inflicted my face on her."

Ortega frowned as though he didn't understand and thought the translation in his head must be bad. "I have

brought her here with me. If you would please allow her to come in and pay her respects…"

Max swallowed hard. This was crazy. Was Señor Ortega making the girl do this? Surely she hadn't really requested this on her own. "I'm sorry," he began. "I'm afraid I can't allow…"

But Renzo had already escorted the girl to the library and she was coming in the door at that very moment. Max braced himself. It wasn't that he was afraid she would scream again. He knew that wouldn't happen. But if he saw horror in her face, he didn't know if he could stand it.

She was so pretty, and so small. As she entered her huge eyes turned on him and he saw the involuntary widening as she took in his face. But almost immediately, her angelic smile took over, and he felt a sense of relief pour through his body.

"Your Highness," she said, with a pretty curtsy. "I am so sorry for scaring you away that day. I cried and cried but my grandfather said not to bother you with such trivial things. But I begged him to let me come to see you again. And here I am."

Max laughed aloud, suddenly as relaxed and happy as he'd been in a long, long time. Could it be that he really wasn't such a monster after all? Was there a chance that he could live a somewhat normal life? Why not? If precious little girls could get over his scars so quickly, why not challenge the rest of the world to do the same?

It was over. Isabella sank into her seat at the end of the table and felt as though she were collapsing like a spent balloon. Her father was sitting with his head in his hands and she wasn't sure if he was crying. Others at the table were shouting and arguing, but she knew there was no more

hope. It was over. The beautiful little restaurant with the special sauces made with *Monta Rosa Basil* was no more. They'd come to meeting after meeting and the result continued to be the same. The mayor, as parliamentarian presiding over this meeting, had finally ruled that her family had to clear out the building in two days.

It was truly over.

Reaching out, she took Luca's hand.

"Come on, Papa," she said sadly. "Let's go."

He looked up and tried to smile at his daughter. "Valentino is coming soon," he said, his voice shaky. "Maybe he will think of something."

She bit back her bitter reply. No recriminations. Reality was what it was. Time to deal with it and move on.

She rose and held out a hand to her father. He looked up but hardly seemed to have the strength to reach for her help. It was truly a sad and hopeless afternoon.

But in that same moment, the double doors to the meeting room swung open abruptly, and a man burst into the room. The reaction swept through the hall like a windstorm. Isabella turned to see who it was, and then couldn't believe her eyes.

There stood a tall, strong, proud man with eyes as black as coal and a presence that made everyone in the room sit up and take notice. It took her a moment to be certain it was Max, because at first she wasn't too sure. There was no hesitation about him, no favoring the good side of his face, no reluctance to challenge the crowd with his standing, scars and all. He was here and he was going to make a difference. That much was obvious.

"Sorry I'm late," he said in a voice that thundered through the room. "I hear you are dealing with a property that I have some interest in, so I decided I'd better be here to help you make the right decision."

The mayor and some of the councilors, after gaping for a few moments, made obsequious gestures and offered their chairs and generally made fools of themselves, and Isabella watched in wonder. He was more regal, more beautiful than ever. Where had this confidence come from? Had it been there all the time and she just hadn't noticed?

Max refused to take a seat. Instead, he stood in the middle of the room where he seemed to be in command of everyone in it. He requested that the mayor read the findings to him, and then the ruling. He listened, frowning, and when it was over he said, "I'm sorry, Mayor Gillano, but I don't agree with your ruling. I have some interest in the restaurant, Rosa, and I want it protected."

Everyone gaped at him in bewilderment. He stared straight ahead at the mayor and went on.

"You see, I'm about to be linked to the Casali family when I marry Isabella Casali. And she in turn will be a partner with me in my extensive real-estate holdings in the village. I believe I hold the lease on the building where you operate your furniture factory, Mayor Gillano. And the apartment building that you manage, Mr. Barelli," he added, looking at the mayor's right-hand man. "Oh, and don't you rent your stables from me, Miss Vivenda?"

He addressed each council member in turn and it seemed his real-estate manager had arranged it so that he had dealings with every one of them.

"Once Isabella is my bride, she will assist me in deciding which leases we may have to break in order to fulfill some new plans we're working on for the village." His gaze swept the room, a slight smile softening the hard lines of his face. "I hope we won't be inconveniencing any of you, but that is always a risk, as I'm sure you are well aware."

The murmurs had a ring of panic to them now. Isabella stared in wonder. She wasn't sure what was happening. Why was Max saying these things? Marrying her? He might have asked first. But she didn't care. She loved watching him and the way he took charge without regard to his scars or how they affected anyone. He'd been born a prince, raised a prince, and he was finally letting his inner prince out.

But what was this business about marrying her? Was this all a ruse, or did he really have something in mind? Her heart was beating so loud, she had to concentrate to understand what he was saying.

"I'm sure this matter can be settled to the benefit of all of us if you will just rescind your ruling regarding the restaurant Rosa." His dark gaze touched every one of them in turn. "Surely the fine can be waived, in light of this new information."

There was utter silence in the room.

He smiled. "Good. That's settled, then. I expect to see the Casali family back over the stove at their restaurant by nightfall."

"Oh, I'm sure something can be arranged..." the mayor was sputtering.

"Oh, yes, indeed," others were saying, suddenly acting as though this had been their intention all along.

Isabella shook her head, her mouth open in astonishment. They all fell into place like bowling pins. The only angry face was Fredo's scowling in the background. But it seemed his wishes were no longer relevant.

Max turned to look at Isabella. She looked at him. Electricity flashed between them, and as though propelled by it, she rose and flew into his arms. He swept her up into the air, and right in front of everyone his mouth came down

on hers and he kissed her as though this were going to be the last kiss in the history of the world.

"I love you, Bella," he whispered close to her ear. "I've found out I can't live without you by my side. Would a wedding fit into your plans?"

"Oh, Max," she sighed, holding him close. "I penciled one in long ago. You're right in step with the program."

"Good," he said, his dark eyes smiling into hers. "You're my conscience and my courage. I need you badly."

"I think you've got the courage all on your own," she responded. "The way you came in here, taking charge, ignoring what they might make of your scars—oh, Max, it was masterful."

"I would never have been able to do something like that if you hadn't started the process of making me face the world," he told her.

The others in the room were still squabbling like a herd of cats, but they were alone in their private oasis, right in the middle of it all.

"Let's get married soon," he said, kissing her again. "We're going to need a very, very long honeymoon."

"Don't worry," she said, laughing as she clung to the man she loved. "I've got plans."

EPILOGUE

MAX stood before a large fountain in a courtyard in Monta Correnti holding a goblet that contained a pinot noir of fabulous vintage. He held it up to the light, enjoying the color, anticipating how it would taste on his tongue. And his mind was full of Isabella.

"Here's to you, my bride-to-be," he muttered, knowing his voice would be covered by the sound of water in the large fountain he stood before. Still, he lowered it further to add, "And to you, my bride that was—my beloved Laura, and our treasured child. You will always be a part of me."

Closing his eyes, he murmured a soft prayer, then smiled as he heard Isabella's voice coming from Rosa, one of two restaurants that bordered the courtyard. She was arguing with her brother, Valentino, again. Those two were at it night and day, it seemed.

They had just finished a wonderful meal to celebrate Luca's birthday and Max had come outside to get some fresh evening air and savor the moment. He'd been happy to be invited to this small, family gathering. Luca seemed to be just about ready to accept that Max was going to marry his daughter.

That was not to say that he was happy about it. He was

very worried that Max would take his daughter away and he would have no one to help him with the restaurant. And in truth, he was right to be worried, Max thought to himself. Right now Isabella was determined to go on helping, knowing what dire straits the finances were in, but there would come a time when she would have to commit fully to him and their relationship. And then—darn right he would take Isabella away.

He turned to look at the other restaurant on the courtyard, Sorella, run by Luca's sister Lisa. Happy diners were coming and going. It was a very popular place. He had yet to try her fare. He would have to do it one of these days. Lisa was a very hands-off manager and her place was doing fine. Surely he and Isabella could hire someone good enough to allow Luca to hand over most of the management in similar fashion.

Glancing back at the Casali place, he saw that Isabella and Valentino were still arguing, but Luca was making his way out onto the courtyard as well—probably fed up with the squabbling. Max chuckled, but turned away and melted into the shadows of the area. He didn't want to get involved in any more Casali family discussions for now. He had a glass of wine to drink and his future happiness to ponder.

Isabella was shaking her head and glaring at her brother. She loved him to distraction, and yet the two of them hardly ever could see eye to eye on anything.

"I wish Cristiano were here instead of being stuck in Australia fighting the brush fires," Luca grumbled as he started out the door onto the courtyard. "He'd knock your two heads together for sure."

"Oh, Papa," Isabella said. "Don't let it bother you. It's as much a family ritual with us as anything." But she turned

right back to Valentino. "You're just so stubborn," she said. "Why don't you just try staying here for a month? Papa would be so happy and—"

"Izzy, why can't you understand? I have a career to think of. I have to defend my position on the tour. I have to fight for every increment of success. It doesn't come easy."

"I can understand that you want to give racing your all, but there is more to life than work, work, work."

"Really? And when did you have this revelation, Cinderella? Remember when we called you that?"

But Isabella had suddenly realized they were alone. "Hey, where did everybody go?" she said, looking around.

"You chased them away with your constant nagging," he teased.

She turned, ready to be outraged, and saw the humor in his eyes. Reluctantly, she smiled back at him. "Okay, I'll leave it alone for now." She sighed, then regained a bit of energy. "Come on. We'll go out in the courtyard, too. It's cooler out there."

They stopped to pour out a glass of wine for each of them, then linked arms and went out into the darkening night. The area was filled with people milling about, but Isabella noticed her father across the way.

"There he is." She frowned, looking harder. "I wonder who that is he's talking to. I don't think it's Max." They started over. "Oh, it's Aunt Lisa," she said as they got closer. "They hardly ever even speak to each other. What in the world…?"

She was about to rush forward when her brother stopped her with a hand on her arm. "There's something about the intensity between them that makes me think we ought to take this carefully," he told her. "Let's go for the side approach. Here, through the bushes."

"I'll ruin my shoes," she protested, but she agreed. There was something odd about the posture between Luca and Lisa that made her want to take it slowly as well. She was naturally protective toward her father. If Lisa was being mean to him, she wanted to be there to take his side—whatever the problem might be. As they drew closer the voices began to be audible. Lisa was the first they heard clearly enough to decipher.

"And here it is, your birthday, and you don't even have your whole family around you, do you?" Lisa was saying, and it was loud enough that anyone who walked past could have heard it.

Isabella made a sound of exasperation and started to push her way out of the bushes to go to her father's aid, but her brother, looking uncomfortable, grabbed her arm again to stop her.

"Shush," he whispered near her ear. "Let's just get out of here."

"But…"

"You've never told them, have you?" Lisa said in a scathing voice. "Here I know more about their brothers than they do."

Brothers? Isabella and Valentino both stopped and turned back, peering through the dim light at their older relatives.

"Lisa, what are you talking about?" Luca demanded. "Have you seen the twins? Have you been to New York?"

His voice was suddenly high-pitched with emotion. Isabella and Valentino looked at each other and they both shrugged at the same time.

"Who are they talking about?" he mouthed to her, and she shrugged again, shaking her head.

"You are the one who should be going to New York, brother dear. You should acknowledge those children you

had so long ago. Don't you realize you've left a huge gaping hole in the middle of your family? You've poisoned relations between your children forever with the actions you've taken. To send those poor little boys away like you did…"

"And why did I have to send them away? You do remember that part of it, don't you, Lisa?"

"Ridiculous."

"It was because you, my loving sister, refused to loan me the money to put food in their mouths. What was I to do? Let them stay here with me and starve?"

She waved a hand in the air. "That's all in the past. You need to take care of the present. You need to contact those boys and try to patch things up." She started to turn away. "Oh, by the way. You do know that Alessandro has a ranch in the West, don't you? And that Angelo is a big baseball star?" She tossed her head, just to show she despised him. "Just thought I'd catch you up on the family news. *Your* family news. Why don't you let the rest of them know about it? I'm sure they'd be interested."

And with that, she turned on her heel and sashayed back toward her restaurant. Isabella waited only a few seconds before bursting out into the opening and going to her father, who looked gray and shaken by the things Lisa had said. He slumped down onto a stone bench and she hurried to his side.

"Papa, what was she talking about?" she said, going down onto one knee before him and searching his face for answers. "Who are these twins she spoke of?"

He looked up at her and winced. "Isabella, Valentino, I have a lot to tell you about. Too much." He gave a heavy sigh. "It's true. I haven't been honest. I've been thinking about it a lot lately and I know I need to fill you in about it all."

"Tell us what, Papa?" She took his hand. "You can tell us anything. You know we love you."

His sigh was deep and heart-rending. "It's the twins. Before I married your mother I had another wife and we had two sons—twins. I haven't seen them since they were little boys." He shook his head.

She squeezed his hand and looked up. "Valentino?" she called, looking for her brother. But he was striding off into the night, as though he wanted almost anything more than to hear about these two new brothers. She stared after him, disappointed again.

She was shocked, but, in a certain corner of her heart, quite thrilled to hear she had two brothers she'd never known about. Though it was a complete surprise, she had to admit there had been hints over the years that there were mysteries in her father's past that she didn't know about. Now she had some confirmation of that. And already she was beginning to formulate the beginning sketches of how she was going to find those twins and bring them home.

That was one thing her aunt Lisa had said that was absolutely right. There did seem to be a gaping hole in the middle of their family. There always had been. She could see that clearly now. And family was everything.

"Max!"

Valentino had deserted her, but at least she could count on Max. She turned as he entered the clearing, reaching for him.

"Oh, Max, hold me," she said. She needed his arms around her. The sand was shifting under her feet again and Max might be the only anchor she had.

She quickly filled him in. "I have two new brothers. How do you like that? And I'm going to make sure they come home soon so we can meet them."

Max nodded, holding her as though he would never let her go. "Sounds like a plan," he said. "Families should be together whenever possible."

She sighed and sank into his embrace. She was so lucky to have him. She knew that her most important responsibilities would be to the new family the two of them would make together and she knew that he felt those ties as deeply as she did. But in the meantime, she needed to shore up her other family where she could. If only her brothers would recognize the truth in that, she thought as she and Max helped her father back to the restaurant, the world would be a better place, especially here in their beloved Bella Rosa.

* * * * *

*Harlequin Intrigue top author Delores Fossen presents
a brand-new series of breathtaking romantic suspense!*
TEXAS MATERNITY: HOSTAGES
The first installment available May 2010:
THE BABY'S GUARDIAN

Shaw cursed and hooked his arm around Sabrina.

Despite the urgency that the deadly gunfire created, he tried to be careful with her, and he took the brunt of the fall when he pulled her to the ground. His shoulder hit hard, but he held on tight to his gun so that it wouldn't be jarred from his hand.

Shaw didn't stop there. He crawled over Sabrina, sheltering her pregnant belly with his body, and he came up ready to return fire.

This was obviously a situation he'd wanted to avoid at all cost. He didn't want his baby in the middle of a fight with these armed fugitives, but when they fired that shot, they'd left him no choice. Now, the trick was to get Sabrina safely out of there.

"Get down," someone on the SWAT team yelled from the roof of the adjacent building.

Shaw did. He dropped lower, covering Sabrina as best he could.

There was another shot, but this one came from a rifleman on the SWAT team. Shaw didn't look up, but he heard the sound of glass being blown apart.

The shots continued, all coming from his men, which meant it might be time to try to get Sabrina to better cover. Shaw glanced at the front of the building.

So that Sabrina's pregnant belly wouldn't be smashed against the ground, Shaw eased off her and moved her to

a sitting position so that her back was against the brick wall. They were close. Too close. And face-to-face.

He found himself staring right into those sea-green eyes.

How will Shaw get Sabrina out?
Follow the daring rescue and the heartbreaking
aftermath in THE BABY'S GUARDIAN
by Delores Fossen,
available May 2010 from Harlequin Intrigue.

Bestselling Harlequin Presents® author

Lynne Graham

introduces

VIRGIN ON HER WEDDING NIGHT

Valente Lorenzatto never forgave Caroline Hales's
abandonment of him at the altar. But now he's
made millions and claimed his aristocratic Venetian
birthright—and he's poised to get his revenge.
He'll ruin Caroline's family by buying out their
company and throwing them out of their mansion…
unless she agrees to give him the wedding night
she denied him five years ago.…

Available May 2010
from Harlequin Presents!

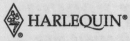

HARLEQUIN®

American ★ Romance®

LAURA MARIE ALTOM

The Baby Twins

Stephanie Olmstead has her hands full raising
her twin baby girls on her own. When she runs
into old friend Brady Flynn, she's shocked to find
herself suddenly attracted to the handsome airline
pilot! Will this flyboy be the perfect daddy—
or will he crash and burn?

"LOVE, HOME & HAPPINESS"

www.eHarlequin.com

HAR75309

LARGER-PRINT BOOKS!

GET 2 FREE LARGER-PRINT NOVELS PLUS
2 FREE GIFTS!

◆ HARLEQUIN®

Romance®

From the Heart, For the Heart

YES! Please send me 2 FREE LARGER-PRINT Harlequin® Romance novels and my 2 FREE gifts (gifts are worth about $10). After receiving them, if I don't wish to receive any more books, I can return the shipping statement marked "cancel." If I don't cancel, I will receive 6 brand-new novels every month and be billed just $4.07 per book in the U.S. or $4.47 per book in Canada. That's a saving of at least 22% off the cover price! It's quite a bargain! Shipping and handling is just 50¢ per book.* I understand that accepting the 2 free books and gifts places me under no obligation to buy anything. I can always return a shipment and cancel at any time. Even if I never buy another book from Harlequin, the two free books and gifts are mine to keep forever.

186/386 HDN E5N4

Name _____ (PLEASE PRINT)

Address _____ Apt. #

City _____ State/Prov. _____ Zip/Postal Code

Signature (if under 18, a parent or guardian must sign)

Mail to the **Harlequin Reader Service:**
IN U.S.A.: P.O. Box 1867, Buffalo, NY 14240-1867
IN CANADA: P.O. Box 609, Fort Erie, Ontario L2A 5X3

Not valid for current subscribers to Harlequin Romance Larger-Print books.

Are you a current subscriber to Harlequin Romance books and want to receive the larger-print edition? Call 1-800-873-8635 today!

* Terms and prices subject to change without notice. Prices do not include applicable taxes. N.Y. residents add applicable sales tax. Canadian residents will be charged applicable provincial taxes and GST. Offer not valid in Quebec. This offer is limited to one order per household. All orders subject to approval. Credit or debit balances in a customer's account(s) may be offset by any other outstanding balance owed by or to the customer. Please allow 4 to 6 weeks for delivery. Offer available while quantities last.

Your Privacy: Harlequin Books is committed to protecting your privacy. Our Privacy Policy is available online at www.eHarlequin.com or upon request from the Reader Service. From time to time we make our lists of customers available to reputable third parties who may have a product or service of interest to you. If you would prefer we not share your name and address, please check here. ☐

Help us get it right—We strive for accurate, respectful and relevant communications. To clarify or modify your communication preferences, visit us at www.ReaderService.com/consumerschoice.

HRLP10R

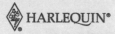
HARLEQUIN®

Showcase

Reader favorites from the most talented voices in romance

Save $1.00 on the purchase of 1 or more Harlequin® Showcase books.

On sale May 11, 2010

SAVE $1.00 on the purchase of 1 or more Harlequin® Showcase books.

Coupon expires Oct 31, 2010. Redeemable at participating retail outlets. Limit one coupon per purchase. Valid in the U.S.A. and Canada only.

52609015

Canadian Retailers: Harlequin Enterprises Limited will pay the face value of this coupon plus 10.25¢ if submitted by customer for this product only. Any other use constitutes fraud. Coupon is nonassignable. Void if taxed, prohibited or restricted by law. Consumer must pay any government taxes. Void if copied. Nielsen Clearing House ("NCH") customers submit coupons and proof of sales to Harlequin Enterprises Limited, P.O. Box 3000, Saint John, NB E2L 4L3, Canada: Non-NCH retailer—for reimbursement submit coupons and proof of sales directly to Harlequin Enterprises Limited, Retail Marketing Department, 225 Duncan Mill Rd., Don Mills, ON M3B 3K9, Canada.

5 65373 00076 2   (8100)0 11651

U.S. Retailers: Harlequin Enterprises Limited will pay the face value of this coupon plus 8¢ if submitted by customer for this product only. Any other use constitutes fraud. Coupon is nonassignable. Void if taxed, prohibited or restricted by law. Consumer must pay any government taxes. Void if copied. For reimbursement submit coupons and proof of sales directly to Harlequin Enterprises Limited, P.O. Box 880478, El Paso, TX 88588-0478, U.S.A. Cash value 1/100 cents.

Coming Next Month

Available May 11, 2010

HRCNMBPA0410